PRAISE FOR
THE CITY UNDER THE BRIDGE

Like her creation Anwyn Baldomyre Laura J Underwood is a bard of major skill. With the first words of "The City under the Bridge" she draws readers into a world of high adventure and daring that they won't want to leave until the tale is told.

— Bradley H. Sinor author of
ECHOES FROM THE DARKNESS and IN THE SHADOWS

~*~

Anwyn Baldmyre is a likable guy haunted by the voice of a nagging, judgmental harp in his head, Glynnanis - the harp- wants the young, careful mage to use his magic more and to strive to reach his full potential. There is a dynamic between the two that's fun to watch unfold while the pair battle corrupt politicos and murderous water ladies as they do battle in the *City Under the Bridge*.

— Selina Rosen author of SWORD MASTERS

~*~

"Laura Underwood spins another delightful story, action-packed and filled with magic, well-written and elegantly told. Recommended!"

— Robin Wayne Bailey author of SWORDS AGAINST THE
SHADOWLANDS

~*~

In Laura J. Underwood's *The City Under the Bridge*, mage-born harper, Anwyn Baldomyre and his harp, Glynnanis, face a foe which can drown a man on dry land. A dangerous creature lurks in the depths of the river and it is Baldomyre's task to find what or who has cursed the people who live in the city under the bridge.
An exciting new story that will be sure to please readers of fantasy everywhere.

— MH Bonham, award-winning author of
LACHLEI, PROPHECY OF SWORDS, RUNESTONE OF TEIWAS, THE
KING'S CHAMPION and SERPENT SINGER

THE CITY UNDER THE BRIDGE

Laura J. Underwood

Wolfsinger Publications Security, Colorado

This book is dedicated to Bards and Harpers Everywhere.

ONE

The sight of the gorge dropping several hundred meters to the rushing river below took Anwyn Baldomyre's breath away. He had heard the thunder of the water well before he crested the rise in the mountain road, but the magnitude of the sound had not prepared him. What lay before him now was so visually stunning, he faltered in his steps.

"Lords and Ladies, Glynnanis, will you look at that," he said.

:*Water*, the harp sang in Anwyn's head, and one note chimed like a rude snort. :*I prefer not to, thank you.*

Anwyn shook his head and smiled. For a creature that had complained about being kept hidden in the dungeons of Far Reach for so long, Glynnanis showed little interest in the natural wonders Anwyn had encountered on his travels through Lamboria.

He sighed and peered across the gorge. "I can't see the other side."

Indeed, a mist as thick as wood smoke hovered over the rim, moving like a crowd of ghosts and making it impossible to tell how high or low the other side might be. *By the Four, I must be up in the clouds!* Alas that meant he did not dare risk using his Gate Song to cross the gorge, not without a clear view of the other side. Rhystar of Far Reach had warned Anwyn the magic song would only safely take the harper some place he had already been, or some place he could see for himself. And since Anwyn could not use each of his magic songs more than once a day, he was not eager to waste this one, much less risk his life.

The road, he noticed, followed this side of the gorge. Perhaps it would lead to a way across as well.

Only one way I'll ever find out.

:*We're going on?* Glynnanis asked.

"I've no desire to go back," Anwyn said. Behind him lay a village he knew would no longer welcome one of silver eyes, even if he had used his limited magic to do them good service. The farther he got from Nymbaria's borders, the more superstitions he found. He glanced at the unicorn head carved from white wood. Glynnanis was eyeing the edge to their right.

:*Then please walk a little closer to the left*, the harp said. :*You know I have no fondness for heights...or water.*

"You have no fondness for anything, I think," Anwyn said with a chuckle then moved that way.

The road stayed on the edge of the cliffs and even began to descend into the gorge. Soon, the cliffs rose like the walls of a great castle, blocking the late afternoon light and plunging the world into bluish shadows. Dark always came earlier to these mountains when one was not atop their snow-clad peaks.

I shall have to find shelter soon, Anwyn thought. The wind that rushed up from the depths of the gorge whipped his cloak into ill-mannered wings and lashed his face with strands of his own hair. It would be impossible to camp in this wind, for no ordinary fire would last.

:Then you should make a magical one, Glynnanis scolded.

"And waste another spell song?" Anwyn retorted. "I'm trying to live as I should, without magic, Glynnanis."

:It is foolish to be so frugal with magic, just because you have not made your sacrifice.

Here we go again. Anwyn rolled his eyes and sighed. The one song that never changed was the harp's constant nagging about Anwyn's refusal to make the sacrifice that would release his power.

:You have great potential, Glynnanis said. *:Why do you waste your skill? You should use your magic. It will teach you to handle it better, and teach you to love it. And eventually, to make the sacrifice that will release your fullest potential as one of the great magister like Rhystar.*

Anwyn frowned and hoped to swiftly find a cave before the temptation to drop Glynnanis in the gorge grew any stronger. But then guilt tightened his gut and banished the thought. Rhystar had made the harp for another who died. He had gifted the harp on Anwyn when his own was burned by the fire wraith that once tortured him.

Anwyn shook those dark memories away, for the road ahead seemed to have no end. As he walked on, watching the shadows grow longer, he saw the gorge bent like an elbow. And as he rounded that turn, he froze.

The gorge widened out ahead, and in that gap, someone had built a massive stone bridge. But it was no ordinary crossing. Its topmost part was a single arch with twin towers and what looked like an opulent palace standing in the middle. He could make out gatehouses and stables and garrisons at each end. Below the span, he saw structures that must have been grand houses or temples, and in the sections below those stood tier upon tier of buildings filling the space from the top to the bottom of the narrowing gorge. In fact, the lower he looked, the more dense and solid the arches and layers were filled. While the structures above were stone and timber, and very lovely, all those below were made of mortared stone and had colorful slate roofs. Many looked as though they had been crammed in haphazardly to form a city gone mad. Tinier and tinier they became until at the very bottom he could see the river boiling out from underneath it all.

"Lords and Ladies," Anwyn exclaimed. To his wonder, a number of people were going about their daily lives, moving in and out of streets barely wide enough to admit a single horse, hanging out of windows and off balconies to shout at one another above the roar of the water. Here and there were terraced patchworks of green where gardens had been coaxed to life. Lanterns that resisted the guttering effect of the fierce wind churned up by the water were being lit along the edges. Laundry flapped in the updraft, like giant birds about to take flight. A warm glow not unlike the first dance of fireflies began to fill the gorge.

"What a wonder this is," Anwyn said. "I hope we can find an inn..."

:*You propose to sleep in that damp, dismal place?* the harp retorted. :*Are you truly so eager to warp me?*

"Oh, Glynnanis, where is your sense of adventure? And anyway, it doesn't look all that dismal."

:*My sense of adventure tells me to stay well away from water*, Glynnanis said. :*And I sense magic here, ancient magic and ill intentions. We should not linger.*

"I sense nothing," Anwyn said. "I think you're just in one of your grumpy moods. Rhystar will be envious when I tell him of this place."

:*Clearly you and I have different ideas of adventure*, the harp said.

Anwyn shook his head and hurried on. Shelter for the night. A sanctuary against wind and water and wolves and bears.

Still, he would make certain Glynnanis was well wrapped.

Just to be safe...

TWO

The road climbed again and eventually brought Anwyn to the height of the span. From here, it was clear the bridge was very wide, though what faced him were small doors in a huge gatehouse, just large enough to admit wagons needing to cross. Already, the wind was filling his nostrils with the scent of food as well as the less pleasant odors some humans sported in their collective dwellings. Now that he stood just at the gates, he did sense something in the rush of the water, a lingering malevolence that ebbed and flowed with the wild river.

:Told you, Glynnanis sang sharply.

Anwyn frowned. Even from here he could see the road he followed ended at this place and picked up on the far side of the bridge. So he had no choice but to follow. He sighed and started on, making for the rise that led to the gatehouse.

The gates were still open, and there were guards standing to either side of that entrance. As Anwyn approached they stepped into his path.

"State your name, your profession and your business in Stonegorge, stranger," the elder of the two said.

"My name is Anwyn Baldomyre, and I am a harper by trade," Anwyn said, and he shifted his cerecloth sack so they could see Glynnanis who remained rigid so as to appear like an ordinary harp. "As to my business—it is to pass through and nothing more. Unless there is an inn within, in which case my business is to spend the night under a roof and go on in the morning."

"Then you must make up your mind," the younger guard said.

"Why?" Anwyn asked.

"The crossing toll is six brass tupins which you must pay on the other side, but those use the inn are allowed to pass over for free," the older guard replied. "Now which shall it be."

"The inn," Anwyn said, hoping it would not prove more expensive than the crossing.

"Very well," the old guard said. "There are three inns within Stonegorge. The Grand View in Upper Stonegorge is five silvers pence a night for a private room, though I think you can get a place in the common room for three. The Middle Arch Inn located in Lower Stonegorge offers private rooms at two silvers each or a place in the common room for five brass tupins. Then down in the Depths, there is the Waterhouse Inn, which offers a private room for a mere two brass tupins a night or a place in the common room for five copper pats."

"Well, then, how do I find this Waterhouse Inn?" Anwyn asked. "My purse is growing thin, I fear."

The guards traded looks. "Surely a harper would prefer to offer his skills at the Grand View or the Middle Arch and receive a fair discount in trade," the older of the pair said.

Anwyn shrugged. "True," he said, "but such a harper is also likely to receive free board in trade for offering to entertain in a place like the Waterhouse."

The older guard looked disturbed. He stepped closer as though not wanting the younger to hear. "Take the advice of an old man," he said softly. "The Depths is no place for a fine youth like yourself. And anyway, there are those who say the Waterhouse is haunted."

"Or cursed," the other muttered, and the elder guard cast a sharp look at the younger to quell his tongue.

"By what?" Anwyn asked.

The guard frowned. "No one is certain, lad, but it drowns men on dry ground, whatever it is. Though some have said it looks like a woman as translucent as air."

Anwyn felt his heart thump a bit to hear that. "Then I shall be careful," he said.

The old guard shook his head and stepped back. "Whatever inn you choose, ask for a token. They will give you one, and when you leave, you present it to the guards at the far end of the bridge. That way, they will know you have spent the night in one of Stonegorge's fine establishments and let you pass."

"Thank you," Anwyn said.

The guards stepped aside and let Anwyn enter the passage under the arches of the gatehouse. Once inside, he saw the stone stairs leading down to the area under the arch. Following that, he entered a grand sort of courtyard. To one side, he saw a series of large pulleys and dangling baskets amid some small daub and wattle and timber shops. At one end, he could see what looked like a small palace. The other end was a stone building whose archway said, "The Grand View." Beautiful, ornate stonework decorated that exterior. To Anwyn's chagrin, music softly floated out of its main doors. So much for trading work for board in that place.

:*We should take the guard's advice*, Glynnanis said. :*The farther we are from the water, the happier I shall be.*

:*I can't afford such a place, and you know it*, Anwyn thought back. It was true. His encounters in the last village had left him a few coins poorer. Granted, he knew he could have opened a gate back to Far Reach and asked Rhystar for a loan. *But the idea is to live within my means by my own wits.* Not to depend on Rhystar for everything he required. Granted, Rhystar would never deny him a penny or a crust, but Anwyn knew he could not let Rhystar keep doing so much for him—no matter how much he loved the old mage.

Anwyn sighed again and looked for the next set of stairs. What he found was a narrow path spiraling downward into the heart of the bridge, so he followed it and made up his mind to seek the Waterhouse Inn, in spite of the guards warnings.

How cursed can it be?

:*I guess we're going to find that out for ourselves, aren't we*, Glynnanis replied.

THREE

Anwyn took several wrong turns in his attempt to find the Waterhouse Inn. For the third time, he stopped under an arch looking out over the water below the bridge, and realized this was where he had already been.

"Lords and Ladies," he muttered. "This place is a veritable maze."

:*A true mage would know how...* Glynnanis began.

:*Oh, be quiet!* he thought. Dark was falling. He knew there would be a full moon tonight, but he had no idea if its light reached into this tangle of alleyways and streets, let alone the depths of the gorge.

He was about to give up and return to the Middle Arch—for he had seen that place in passing above—when a small boy stepped out of the shadows looking furtively about.

"Sir," the lad said. "Could you spare a copper pat?"

The lad was thin, all arms and legs wrapped in rags. His face was pale and smudged. An urchin of the streets, Anwyn thought. He had met many in his travels. This one lacked the mean glint in his blue eyes, though, and Anwyn sighed.

"I say, I'll give you two copper pats if you'll show me the way to the Waterhouse Inn," Anwyn said.

The urchin's eyes lit up with fear. "I know the way, but, if I show you, will you promise not to let the Water Lady have me?"

"The Water Lady?" Anwyn repeated. "Who is...?"

"Here now, what are you up to!" a gruff voice shouted. The urchin squeaked and bolted for the shadows. Anwyn turned with a glower as a large man in a billowing blue cloak and matching over tunic charged up the cobbles. He waved a cudgel with a brass head on the end. "I'll toss you over the rails into the river when I find you, boy!"

The burly man stepped closer.

"Are you all right, sir?" he asked, looking down at Anwyn as though assessing his worth.

Anwyn took a deep breath, swallowing his anger. This clod was much larger than he, and his cudgel was waving too close for comfort. "I'm fine," Anwyn said, "though I must admit I am a little disappointed that you frightened my guide."

"Your guide, young sir?" the man said. "Your doom, more likely. These urchins often ply strangers for a pat or two, and then lead them into dark alleys where they will be beaten and robbed by a dozen or so of his kith and kin."

Anwyn stopped his tongue from blurting, *And what stops a bully like you from doing the same?*

"So, where were you headed, sir? Looking for a bit of pleasure in the Depths?"

"No," Anwyn said. "I was looking for an inn called the Waterhouse, and that lad was going to lead me there."

"I can lead you there, sir."

"And just who are you?" Anwyn asked.

"Gordon the Watchman," the man said and held up his cudgel so Anwyn could see the brass band with the insignia about one end. "Hired by Lord Maladar himself."

"Lord Maladar?"

"Him what rules in Stonegorge," Gordon said.

"Very well, then," Anwyn said. "Where is this inn?"

"I'll have to lead you there," Gordon said and held out his hand. "Five coppers and I'll take you all the way to the door."

"Five coppers?"

"It's time off me duties, sir," Gordon said. "They takes my pay if I leave my duties..."

"Five coppers," Anwyn muttered, and reluctantly dug them free of his satchel. He laid them in Gordon's meaty hand.

"This way," Gordon said as he slipped the coins into his own pouch. He turned and started back into the darkest looking areas Anwyn had been purposely avoiding. Reluctantly, Anwyn followed.

Gordon proved good as his word—or his price—for the dark area hid the stairs Anwyn had been seeking. Still uncertain, he followed the watchman down that flight of stairs and into the warren that made up the Depths. *This place is aptly named*, Anwyn thought. Gordon led Anwyn into the very heart of the Stonegorge and beyond, it seemed. Their lamp-lit path wound in and out among slumps of stone buildings that upon close examination looked seedier and less solid than they had from above. Indeed, here and there Anwyn saw signs stone had been added in just to shore up the existing structures. The color of the stone was light grey compared to the darker moist stones that made up most of this bridge. Cracks were visible too, and water was everywhere. The cobbles here were broken, and puddles and trickles of moisture claimed much of the space, often forcing Anwyn to hop to keep his boots dry. The denizens of these parts were common folk, dressed more drably than those he had seen above. A few even looked at him as though he was mad to enter this place.

He was starting to think that himself, though not so Glynnanis would hear. He would have to remember to call his Song of Warmth to keep the harp dry.

Gordon the Watchman suddenly stopped and gestured to a doorway set back into a short courtyard behind one of the support pillars of stone that Anwyn encountered on his way down. Above the arch was a sign made of stone, and carved on its surface was "The Waterhouse Inn." The rush of the river sounded as though it were right next to Anwyn's head. Gordon held out his hand expectantly, and frowning, Anwyn gave him another copper pat—praying he would have enough to spend the night—and stepped up to the door. The hour was still early enough the door was not barred. He pushed into a dark room where the light of the lanterns muted everything with dull amber, and glittered off the walls. A deep breath revealed the odors of men, food and much moisture in the air.

:*This will warp me!* Glynnanis sang.

:*Quiet!* he thought and resisted the urge to shake the harp sack in frustration.

A few heads turned towards him. He wondered if any of them could hear Glynnanis' voice. But he saw no sign of grey or silver eyes, though in this light, it was admittedly not easy to tell. Some merely looked curious, others relieved. He threaded his way among the quiet mutters of the folk who sat nursing their ales and their meals, noticing some eyes followed him as he stopped at the bar.

Supplies were everywhere, tuns of ale, barrels of salt fish, and many other items that would normally have been down in the stores were crammed in as close as safely possible to a hearth where a fire burned and a pot bubbled with thick soup that smelled delicious. The whole arrangement left a narrow space in the crowded gap behind the bar, but the occupant moved up and down as though there was nothing in her way. She was a woman with a thin worn face haloed by a frazzle of wispy white hair escaping from her long braid, and as she dashed back and forth, she ordered a potboy and a thin young man about. Her eyes reminded Anwyn of a sparrow when she looked up. She even managed a smile that made him think of a sprite.

"Welcome to the Waterhouse Inn, stranger," she said. "What can I do for you?"

"A room," Anwyn said, "and I wondered if I could barter my services in exchange. And the guards said to ask you for a token."

"Ah, just passing through, then," she said. "Why certainly. I'm Olena, proprietress of this old place, so if you barter with any, it will be me. What skills, pray tell, do you have to offer in trade?"

Anwyn pulled back the cover to reveal Glynnanis. Olena's white brows rose in admiration. The potboy dropped one of the cups in astonishment, and she cast the lad a scolding glance. "Go on, Linden, clean it up."

The lad rushed off to obey. That was when Olena leaned closer to Anwyn and whispered, "You might want to reconsider staying at the Middle Arch Inn in Lower Stonegorge. With a beautiful instrument like that you might not want to risk the damp doing it harm."

She cast a quick look over her shoulder as she spoke. The tall thin youth was busy watching a pair of doxies who sat with a couple of men. Longing filled his eyes. "Greeley, don't stand there like a lump staring at those girls," Olena said sharply. "Finish drying those mugs."

Greeley ducked his head in shame and hastened to do as he was bid. Embarrassed, Anwyn turned from him to look at the walls of stone that stood behind Olena's bar and saw the rivulets of moisture that crept down the stones of the wall. So that was the diamond-like glitter.

"I am certain my instrument and I will be fine," Anwyn said. "That is why it wears a cerecloth sack."

"Very well," she said, and just a hint of sadness softened her expression. "Let us hear a song from you, and then we will decide."

Anwyn bowed slightly and took a seat beside the bar. He drew Glynnanis free of the sack and raked the golden strings with skilled fingers. His music rang sweet, and the malaise that hung in the air seemed to fade in response. He started out with a sweet straspey then moved into a gentle jig. Some hands began to clap a rhythm to his song. Some heads nodded time. Mistress Olena smiled gleefully, for the music cheered her patrons and brought more orders for her ale. Even the lights seemed brighter when Anwyn finally ceased to play.

Mistress Olena clapped her hand. "You are a wonder, young man," she said. "May I know your name?"

"I am Anwyn Baldomyre," he said.

"Well, Master Baldomyre, you have earned my best room for that," she said. "And I will throw in a meal if you play a bit more."

Anwyn nodded his head respectfully and said, "It will be my pleasure."

FOUR

Anwyn felt pleased with his own work that night. He had always been partial to entertaining common folk, for they seemed more grateful of his skills. *Men with small purses and little coin enjoy music more because it is free*, he thought. And while he had entertained in great halls, he liked how his music made those of lesser means happy.

By the time he stopped playing, the inn was a lively place. Men and women danced and laughed and some even tossed him coppers to show their appreciation. As their numbers thinned, Anwyn felt his purse grow heavier.

Finally, Mistress Olena offered to fix him a bowl of the soup she kept simmering, and added bread and cheese to the fare. Anwyn devoured them, uncertain why his appetite felt so strong The food was good, and he felt much more welcome than he had in a while.

Once he had filled his belly, Mistress Olena gathered a lantern and led him to the chambers. There were no windows in the passageway, and the walls did exude a dampness that seemed unnatural. She shouldered open a wooden door warped by the moisture that hung in the air, and let him see into the room.

He would not call it the best he had seen, but it was large enough to accommodate a bed, a table and a chair, and the reeds on the floor looked newly placed. There was even a small fireplace off to one side. *At least we will be warm*, he thought. A tall window occupied the wall opposite the door. When Anwyn peered out, he was startled to see how close to the river he stood. Great gouts of white water were running from under the floors beneath his feet. He could feel the rumble of its passage like a low thrum on a harp string.

"Is it always this swift and high?" he asked, drawing back inside to watch his hostess move around to light the fire and make sure all was to perfection.

She paused from turning down the blankets and glanced over her shoulder. "No," she said. "There was a time I could actually get into my cellars without fear of being swallowed by the river. But it seems like for the last two moons it has been rising. Our good lord has tried to blame it on the seasons, but this was a mild winter compared to some we've had. And anyway, the fishing is not what it used to be. There was a time that those who dwelled in the depths were great fishermen. No more."

"Ah, I wondered why all the barrels and crates were up in the inn," Anwyn said. "I thought it might be that folks were afraid to enter the cellar."

She frowned. "Why would you think that?" she asked.

"Well, the old guard at the gate seemed to think this place was haunted by a translucent woman," Anwyn said.

:Don't forget cursed, Glynnanis said. *:I'm certainly cursing all this moisture. Get me away from this window, please!*

Anwyn bit his tongue and tried not to swear at the harp. He sat Glynnanis over in the chair.

Olena sighed. "I shall have to have words with old Hannon about his gossiping guards for that. He has trained them better than to tell idle tales to potential customers. Business has been bad enough as it is without the fish."

"The fish are gone?" Anwyn said and glanced out the window again. "As swift as that water runs, how could any man fish here?"

"Oh, one used to be able to catch hundreds of them by spreading nets in the spring when they move up river to spawn, and late in the year when they return to the sea," she said. "Indeed, Stonegorge once made its fortune on the fish. It is how our good lord Maladar's ancestors made his family wealthy and built Stonegorge. But now—the nets are torn regularly in the rush of water, and the fish all get away, I suppose. It is why they started taking such a high toll from travelers—the city coffers, some say, are nearly dry. So of course, men will talk of curses and monsters and haunting when they cannot find anything else to blame for their ills..."

"He seemed rather intent on warning me," Anwyn said. "Something about men drowning on dry ground."

Her shoulders rounded in defeat. "Well...you should not have anything to worry about, Master Anwyn" she said. "Just keep the windows latched and the fire going, and you won't be bothered."

Anwyn frowned. "By what?" he asked. "What distresses this place so?"

"If I knew, I would find someone to stop it," she said. "Now, you should rest and not concern yourself, young Anwyn. Oh, here." She reached into her apron pocket and drew out a flat stone with a mark on it. "Your token. You will need it when you leave tomorrow. Thank you for entertaining my guests and regulars."

She turned and started for the door.

"Mistress," he called.

She paused and looked back.

"If there is anything I can do," he ventured.

She shook her head and smiled wanly. "There is nothing you can do," she said, and before he could question her further, she slipped out of the room and closed the door.

Anwyn frowned and turned back to look out the window again. He stared at the hypnotic fury of the water as the last of the light began to face in the west. Hints of spray touched his face, damp fingers that tickled and moistened his hair.

:Must you always do what you are told not to do? Glynnanis asked.

"What do you mean?" Anwyn asked, not fearing he would be heard between the water and the stone walls.

:She told you to latch the window, didn't she?

"I will," Anwyn said.

:You could fall in, the harp said.

"Would you care if I fell in, Glynnanis? Since you think I waste my life?"

:Well, of course, I would care, Glynnanis sang indignantly. *:I don't expect I'll grow legs again any time soon.*

Anwyn chuckled. Leave it to the harp to have some practical reason for not wanting his demise. He drew back, closing the window and sliding the bolt into place. Water dappled the warped diamonds of glass. Anwyn shook water from his hair and walked over to stand before the fire, stretching hands to the warmth.

"If you could grow legs, Glynnanis, would you carry me?" Anwyn asked playfully. "Considering all the leagues I have carried you, I should like to ride."

:Don't be foolish. Rhystar would never consider adding legs to a harp. He knows I would have run away from those dungeons he kept me in for so long...

"Rhystar didn't keep you in a dungeon, Glynnanis. He had you in the store room, covered and protected."

:As long as I was there, it was a prison, the harp said. *:Why do you think I was glad you decided to leave Far Reach and take me with you when Rhystar asked you to deliver that message?*

How long had that been? Seemed like Anwyn had left Far Reach years ago now. Longer still since he said goodbye to his family and left home. How he missed them all. His father, his mother, his siblings...Rhystar. But home would always be a place of sad memories. Only Far Reach and its master brought comfort now. Anwyn sighed and turned back, intending to sit on the bed and pull off his boots.

He froze.

A shape stood at the window, a translucent form that might have been a woman. Her hands and face pressed against the panes as though trying to see who was inside. Anwyn gasped and jerked back, and the form vanished, leaving naught but moist handprints and rivulets of water running down the outside of the glass that sloughed off in a cascade of liquid.

"Did you see that?" Anwyn asked.

:See what? Glynnanis asked. *:You turned me away so I cannot see the window at this moment—not that I am ungrateful. Looking at water bothers me, you know.*

"Never mind," Anwyn said then hurried over to the window to draw the tapestry drapes and shut out the memory of the sight. "I guess I am just tired. The moon is reflecting on the water and on the glass. Nothing more."

He sat on the bed and pulled off his boots and lay back, not bothering to extinguish the lights. As if to prove him right, he fell almost immediately to sleep.

FIVE

Frantic shouts of terror and outrage woke Anwyn from his sleep. The stone walls of the inn echoed with a cacophony of voices. He sat up on the bed, grabbed his boots and pulled them on. Then grabbing his cloak and Glynnanis, he hurried for the door.

The center of confusion was in the common room. As he hurried down the corridors and into that chamber, he spied a number of folk gathered around the center of the room.

"Get back, all of you, there is nothing here to see," a man ordered.

Anwyn held his spot as the occupants thinned, leaving him a better view. Mistress Olena was on the floor at someone's side. Standing over her was the greedy wretch of a watchman, Gordon. He looked sharply at Anwyn and frowned.

"I said to get back," Gordon said.

"Oh, Gordon, don't be such a grouch," Olena said and she glanced up. "Between you and Captain Hannon's guards, it is a wonder I have any guests at all."

"Beg pardon, I did not mean to intrude, but I was awakened by all the commotion," Anwyn said.

He stepped closer as he spoke, then paused when he saw it was young Greeley who lay sprawled on the reeds. His head was turned and he was streaming water across his bluish lips.

"What happened to him?" Anwyn asked.

"Nothing of concern to..."

"He drown," Mistress Olena said, rising to her feet and glowering at Gordon. "As so many others have."

Anwyn frowned. "How can a man drown and be dry?" he asked, pointing to Greeley's clothes. Indeed, the only water on him was that slipping from between his lips.

"Were you not told about the monster that dwells in these parts?" Gordon asked. "The dreaded water lady?"

"Gordon, please stop it," Olena said. "Go fetch some men and a stretcher to take Greeley to his mother. And you'd best be gentle when you tell her what became of her son or you'll answer to me."

Gordon hesitated, and for a moment, Anwyn wondered if the man would put forth his hand. Instead, he shrugged his cloak close to him and hurried for the main door. Mistress Olena went behind the bar and rummaged up a blanket and brought it back. Anwyn assisted her in covering the corpse.

"I am sorry you had to see this," she said in a distracted manner. "No doubt, you will leave and tell men that it is not safe to stay here."

"Why would I do that?" Anwyn asked.

Olena fixed him with her bird-like stare. "You are not afraid?"

"Of course, I am afraid," Anwyn said with a half smile. "I am afraid of many things. But I think I saw this water lady tonight."

"Where?"

"At my window," he said.

Olena sighed and sat down in one of the chairs that were scattered about. "I had hoped you would not see her. I had hoped tonight would be different. Your music made them forget, you know."

"Forget what?" Anwyn asked. "What is happening here?"

"I wish I knew," she said, shaking her head. "This inn has been in my family for seven generations now. It started out as no more than a few rooms over the water, but then my grandfather got the idea that it should be larger. In spite of being told he was mad, he turned it into a successful house with a good reputation for inexpensive rooms."

"Considering the price of the toll to cross this place," Anwyn said, "it was good of him to think of the travelers."

"My father—it was he who pushed to get the tokens of free passage to those who stayed the night. He thought it would encourage more merchants and travelers to stay here a while, which would put more money in the hands of the businesses here. Of course, in his days, the toll was but two brass tupins a head. And Stonegorge was profitable, even for those dwelling in the Depths. My father raised my brother to take over this place after him so it would continue in our family. But his plans never came to pass, and when he died twenty years ago, it was I who became mistress of the Waterhouse."

"What happened to your brother?"

"He was a good man, my brother—perhaps too good for his own sake," Olena said. "He died when he tried to save a fisherman who had become tangled in his own net. My brother nearly had the man up on the dock when my brother slipped and fell in and was swept away by the river. They found his body washed ashore some leagues to the south."

"I'm sorry," Anwyn said.

"Don't be. It was long ago, and I have long since gotten over my grief. I gladly settled into my duties as the innkeeper, and all was well. But then, fifteen years ago, Lord Maladar married a lady from the north. Cold-hearted she was—and greedy for all the fineries a woman thinks she must have. As I heard it, she drained my lord's coffers, forcing him to raise the toll. She tried to abolish the tokens as well, saying those of us who owned inns were stealing from his lordship's purse, but that system was too firmly in place. So then she forced his lordship to force the innkeepers to raise their rates, and she made us pay for the tokens themselves. We could not refuse, for all who have traveled through Stonegorge know that spending a night earned them free passage. Little do they know, if they stay in one of the inns above, they actually pay for the toll."

She went quiet, and Anwyn heard the surly grunts of men entering the inn. He turned and watched as Gordon stood back ordering a couple of youths to make haste. Then Gordon came over and thrust out his hand expectantly. Mistress Olena bristled.

"Since when must we pay the watch to do its chores?" she asked.

"It's not for me," Gordon said with a sneer, "but for these lads I had to roust from their beds to come carry the unfortunate home to his mother..."

Mistress Olena looked as though she did not believe him. Still, she extracted herself from the chair and walked over behind the bar. Anwyn watched her duck down, and noticed Gordon strain to look over the wood and see where she was. She popped up quite suddenly and slapped a pair of copper pats down on the counter.

"There," she said. "A copper for each man."

"Would not two per man be more generous?" Gordon asked.

Anwyn saw one of the sleepy youths roll his eyes.

"One each man is more than sufficient," Olena replied. "Or shall I ask Captain Hannon to speak with you on the matter of trying to graft old ladies?"

Gordon stiffened and a dark sneer curled his lips back. He snatched up the two coppers and thumped out the door in the wake of the men carrying the corpse. Olena stayed where she was only until the door closed. Her fierce demeanor diminished as she wandered back to her place across from Anwyn.

"I grow too old for these contests of will with that one," she said wearily and shook her head.

Anwyn nodded. "He managed to frighten a lad off that was going to show me the way here for two coppers, then demanded five to lead me here."

"You should not have paid him," she said. "It's worse than the toll. I sometimes think Gordon is the eyes and ears of the she-wolf who rules from above. Sometimes I wonder if it were not *her* fault when three moons ago the river rose and became too hostile even for the fish. It would be just like her to do so just to drive us from the Depths."

"What really happened?" Anwyn asked. "A storm? Heavy snows?" He so hoped the explanation was a logical one.

"Oh that it were so simple," Olena said. "But no, that is when the Water Lady first came. From where or even what she really is, I cannot say. It started when the cellars of the bottom-most dwellings began to flood a little more each day, as though the water was flowing through every crack it could find. Then some of the foundations started to shift, and suddenly there was a river washing through where my cellars had been. But of course, what threatened my inn threatened the very foundations of Stonegorge, so his lordship had men bring down stone to try and repair what the river had done. But no matter how much they brought down, more water came in—and with the water's rise, the strange deaths began. And the rumors of a woman as translucent as water began to spread."

"But who is she?" Anwyn asked.

:*Wouldn't what be a better questions?* Glynnanis sang to his mind.

Anwyn flinched. Mistress Olena was looking at her hands and did not see. She merely shrugged.

"Some think she is a water spirit, or a river spirit tired of our company. Others believe she is the spirit of the sorceress of the north, come to punish us for stealing stones from her deserted keep."

"A sorceress?"

"It's just a mad rumor," Olena said. "No one believes those old stories any more about witch folk and strange monsters and some silver man who attacked Lamboria during the ancient wars over in the mountains on the borders."

Anwyn held his tongue. It was one reason magic was so ill received in many parts of Lamboria. Did Olena even know what his silver eyes meant? He put a finger to a whorl in the wood of the table and traced it.

"So the stones in this place came from the keep of this long dead sorceress?" Anwyn said. "Just where is this place?"

Olena fixed him with a maternal scowl. "Don't you be thinking of going there, laddie," she said. "It's no place for decent folk. But yes, it is the place where they say the stone came from."

"And who would know more about this?"

She shrugged. "Captain Hannon might. I seem to recall he was the one who convinced his lordship of the urgency of finding stone to deal with the water and the supports."

"And where would I find Captain Hannon?"

"In his bed at this hour," Olena said. "Wait until tomorrow, young Anwyn. Sleep tonight. The creature has had her fill, I am sure. Tomorrow, you can go topside and speak to Hannon, and while you're at it, you can tell him about that bully Gordon robbing you of copper pats just to lead you to my inn."

Anwyn smiled. "I shall do as you ask," he said.

But he was not certain as he left the table and headed back for the solitude of his room, that he would get much sleep.

The sound of the rushing water lulled Anwyn to sleep. More than once as the rest of the night passed, he awoke in the deep dark, thinking there was someone nearby. But when he opened his eyes and scanned the chamber in the dull light of the last embers of his fire, there was nothing to be seen.

So he felt a little groggy when he rose the next morning; and was not surprised to see his hostess looking no more alert when he washed his face in the chilly water of the ewer and sauntered back to the common room to seek breakfast. Still, Olena greeted Anwyn with a cheery smile that hid the dark deeds of last night. The potboy—Linden—was at the counter helping her with the customers who slipped in for a morning meal.

Today, Anwyn saw travelers who had stayed overnight. Precious few, he noted, and among them the surly-faced Gordon was stuffing his face on boiled eggs and cheese and bread he tore apart with his huge hands.

He glanced briefly at Anwyn then at his own meal and pretended he had not even noticed the harper there.

Anwyn shook his head and stepped over to the bar. Olena almost immediately set a tray of eggs, bread and cheese before him. "Help yourself," she said merrily, so Anwyn took one of the eggs and a chunk of cheese and a bit of bread. He stood by, devouring them as the potboy handed over a mug of what looked like watered ale. Anwyn managed not to frown. He knew humans drank the stuff day and night, but in the morning, he would rather have something else.

But he drank it and found it was not as bitter as some he had tested in his journey. More like a sweet cider. He drained it gladly then smiled as he set the mug aside.

"Good mistress Olena," he announced. "I thank you for the hospitality of your house. I shall sing of its praises for many a year, I am sure."

The compliment made her beam, and several of the locals raised their mugs and said, "Hear, hear..."

Anwyn swept a bow to all and hurried for the door. He was not surprised to see Gordon's eyes follow him.

SIX

Olena had told Anwyn the baskets he had seen dangling from wooden arms above on the north side of Stonegorge were there to take a man swiftly to the top. Since the climb had no appeal—and would likely take most of the day—he took her advice and made his way towards the far side of the little city. It was easy enough to traverse in the daylight, and he could see all the puddles. There were more people too, tradesmen and fishermen and housewives doing laundry. It occurred to him this would be a fascinating place to explore.

:*If you don't mind being drown?* Glynnanis said.

There was that, Anwyn would agree. He continued through the streets, looking occasionally at tiny shops and doorways.

:*We're being followed*, Glynnanis suddenly said.

By whom? Anwyn thought.

:*By that great goon Gordon, of course*, the harp replied.

Gordon? Anwyn paused as though adjusting the strap of his satchel and glanced back over his shoulder. Sure enough, Gordon stopped, looking into a barrel as though it contained some great mystery.

And just what does he want? Anwyn wondered.

He picked up his pace, though not so it looked like he was trying to escape. After all, Gordon was a watchman, if a greedy one, and he likely had others of his profession within calling distance. So Anwyn kept going as though unconcerned, winding through the streets until at last he found the docks and the wide strip of the lower market Olena had spoken of, and the baskets as well.

By the Four, he thought as he reached the open archways.

Before him stretched a long platform reached by rows of stairs through the archways and sitting higher to keep the river from spilling over its edge and into the streets of The Depths. A market had been set up there, and already folks were up and about hawking their wares. Smaller docks and stone jetties jutted out into the rush of the river where the fishermen plied their trade. The baskets, it seemed were exactly what she said. Large enough to hold several men, they rose on ropes and pulleys, dragged by donkeys tied into walking a circle and turning a great wheel. Anwyn stepped out on one of the jetties, and turning away from the river, he leaned back, trying to see the top of the bridge, wondering if he was going to be able to manage riding up that dizzying height.

:*It's one or the other*, Glynnanis suggested. :*Ride or walk back to the stairs.*

"No, not the stairs," Anwyn muttered quietly. He could see Gordon lurking by one of the openings, hands locked behind him as he glanced here and there.

He's not very good at subterfuge, Anwyn thought and heard the harp chuckle in his head.

With a sigh, Anwyn walked over to where some men were sitting about. "Excuse me," he said. "Where does one inquire about riding the baskets up to the top?"

One of the men pointed to a small kiosk near one of the docks. "Pay for yer tokens there," he said.

Anwyn nodded and crossed the stone docks. He glanced up river and was impressed to see that the water cascaded rapidly over a multitude of gigantic stones. Spray moistened the air, and as before, he noticed the water was high. Reaching the kiosk, he found an elderly man who took his six coppers and gave him a token and told him to give it to someone standing near one of the baskets just as it landed. Thanking him, Anwyn walked over and had to wait as others disembarked. He showed his token and was admitted to the basket.

Its sides were high and well woven, and there was a bench around the edge. Above the seats but below the rims were windows that one could peer through, so he quickly claimed a place and settled down. Two others stepped onboard, claiming the seats across the way. The fourth side of the basket was closed and tied shut. Then the basket lurched heavily and suddenly began to rise. Anwyn's gasp of surprise gained him mild glances of bemusement from his fellow passengers.

He looked through the window and watched as they ascended. As the basket rose, he could see farther upriver and on into the gorge. Small waterfalls tumbled as far as the eye could see, and their mist rose to obscure and haze some of the mountains beyond. He could see where the road continued north, and where it split and went two ways: one inland, and the other continuing to follow the river.

The basket lurched again, and was dragged clumsily to one side. Anwyn sat down, his knuckles white as they grasped the bench beneath him, for it seriously felt as though they were going to tip. But instead, the basket's crane was pulled inward. Its doorway was opened, and he saw he was not actually at the top yet. The two men piled out and another looked in. "Well, lad, this is as far as it goes," he said.

"But I thought it went to the top," Anwyn said.

The man shook his head. "Above us is the palace and only Lord Maladar and her Ladyship are allowed to ride the baskets up there. We're as high as you can go in Upper Stonegorge. If you want to go topside, you must walk the rest of the way. Sorry, lad. The walk will do ye good."

Anwyn pulled himself out of the basket. "Can you tell me where I might find Captain Hannon?"

"Can't say as I know the name," the man said, "but if he's a captain, he's likely to be in the garrison topside."

Anwyn thanked the man and hurried towards the stairs. He had to climb two sets, cut across and climb one more before he emerged in that open area atop the bridge.

There were guards everywhere, mostly lined up along the stone walls looking outward. *Surely one of them will know where Hannon is*, he thought. So he walked over to the nearest one and asked.

The guard pointed towards the Eastern end of the bridge. Anwyn had to walk under the grand archway that cut through the palace itself. Here there were iron gates across passages that would lead into the keep proper, and those were heavily guarded as well. He passed them by, peering at the fancy stone work of gargoyles and relief carvings of warriors as he made his way towards the far end where the gatehouse garrisons stood.

More inquiries finally got him directed to a stable on one side. He walked in, seeing a number of men about. They watched as two men traded blows with quarterstaffs, moving up and down the stable rows. Anwyn stopped where he was and watched the feverish display. The men danced back and forth, staffs filling the air with the clatter of wood. One of them clearly had the advantage, for his staff always seemed to be able to get past the attempts to block. Anwyn had watched his own sibling spar this way enough to know skill when he saw it, so he waited.

The quicker man suddenly managed to hook his staff behind the ankle of the other and sent him crashing to the floor. Anwyn held his breath as the victor's staff then landed gently on the loser's throat. "Yield?" the victor called.

"To you, Captain, of course," the loser said.

"You should not yield just because I am your commander, lad."

The victor drew back, pulling off his helmet to reveal a long white mustache and lengthy white hair. Laugh wrinkles ringed his eyes. Anwyn stepped closer and added his applause to that of the men who were cheering. A few of them turned looked at him and frowned.

"Are you lost, stranger?" the victor asked before anyone else could.

"Sorry, I did not mean to intrude, but I seek Captain Hannon," Anwyn said.

"Ah," the loser said as he pulled off his helmet. He was clearly a younger man, and as he rose to his feel, he smiled. "Sergeant Throm at your service. Why would you be looking for our captain? He's a rather busy man, you know."

A couple of the others chuckled. The younger winked at the elder.

"Because Mistress Olena of the Waterhouse Inn said he might be able to assist me."

The old man's expression changed from a frown to a soft look of puzzlement. "Then I am Captain Hannon," he said. "Is the mistress of the Waterhouse all right?"

"Yes, she is well," Anwyn said, "though a bit tired, I think. And not terribly happy about the loss of one of her employees."

Captain Hannon frowned again. "Come with me, lad," he said and turning on his heels, he started back deeper into the stables. "I'll catch the rest of you later. Sergeant Throm, see that the watches are being carried out."

"Yes, Captain," Sergeant Throm said and turned to draw the others from the area.

Anwyn watched them leave and frowned when he thought he saw a flash of familiar blue outside the stable door. *Lords and Ladies, what is Gordon up to now?* Anwyn thought. With a shake of his head, he hurried after the old man.

SEVEN

The stables connected to a barracks. Captain Hannon led Anwyn through a chamber where a number of men slept on cots and pallets. A few of them wiled away their time playing games of chance. Still others practiced with quarterstaffs and halberds.

At the far end, Hannon passed through a door that opened into a smaller office. "Wait here, and I'll only be a moment," Hannon said. He continued to move through to yet another door where a bedchamber was revealed. The door closed and Anwyn sank into a chair before a table that served as Hannon's desk.

:*This is a waste of time*, Glynnanis said. :*We should be on our way instead of asking this man silly question.*

:*And who says they're silly questions?* Anwyn thought.

:*Just what are you thinking?* Glynnanis asked.

Anwyn sighed. :*I am thinking that I know what that creature is.*

:*Oh, and what would that be?* Glynnanis challenged.

Before Anwyn could reply, Captain Hannon returned. He walked over and seated himself behind the table.

"We can speak freely here," Hannon said. "Now perhaps you should begin by telling me who you are and why Mistress Olena sent you? And while you are at it, what is this about a man dying last night?"

"I think the unfortunate's name was Greeley, sir," Anwyn said. "Apparently he drowned, though the only evidence was that he was streaming as a man who had been in the water would." Anwyn shuddered as he recalled he had seen drowned men stream before. Never a pleasant sight. "As to why Mistress Olena sent me, she thought you might be able to provide me with information concerning the origin of the stones being used to repair the cracks in the walls near her inn. And I am Anwyn Baldomyre, a harper by trade."

Captain Hannon leaned back and steeple his fingers in thought. "Why are you so concerned about where we obtained the stone?" he asked.

"Because I think it is why the creature is there."

Hannon frowned. "The creature? Then you have seen the Water Lady?"

"She was at my window last night," Anwyn said. "I could see the moonlight through her, and she left water on the glass."

"Indeed," Hannon said. "Well, to answer your question, the stone came from the ruins of a keep to the north of here, a little over a league away. When I told Lord Maladar we needed to do something to stop the crumbling and cracking of the foundations of Stonegorge, his lady suggested we take stones from that keep."

"His lady?"

"Lady Rena, his wife," Hannon said. "I dare say if she had not been so gracious as to intervene, his Lordship would have done nothing."

"How is that?" Anwyn asked.

"What do you mean?"

"Well, from what Mistress Olena said, the Lady is the reason for the financial hardships of Stonegorge. Why would she take the time to suggest a place for gathering stone?"

Hannon shook his head and smiled faintly. "Olena has never been fond of Lady Rena. But yes, it was the Lady who suggested we use stone from the keep. She came from the north, and she knew of its presence. Said it was deserted. She even checked on the workers who carted the stone down and put it into place. And once, for amusement, she actually threw a stone into one of the pillars so she could say she was doing her part to preserve Stonegorge."

"Are you saying Olena lies?" Anwyn asked.

He jumped when Captain Hannon slammed a fist on the table. "Never ever say I would call Olena a liar!" Hannon snapped. "She is a decent and honest woman, and were I not Captain of the Guard, I would gladly move into the Waterhouse and help her take care of it."

Anwyn drew back, expecting the man to strike him. Captain Hannon took a deep breath and sat back down.

"My apologies," he said. "I am sure Mistress Olena told you I was a surly bear."

Anwyn shook his head, fighting the urge to smile. "She spoke highly of you."

That remark drew the last of the frown from Hannon's rugged features. His mustache twitched. "Did she really? Well. Was there anything else I could do for you?"

"No thank you," Anwyn said. "Unless you can tell me exactly where this old keep is."

"Follow the river road north, lad, and you can't miss it." Hannon arched an eyebrow. "But why would you want to go there, lad?"

"To satisfy my own curiosity," he said.

"Curiosity should be tempered with caution," Hannon said.

:*That's what I keep telling you*, Glynnanis said.

"I will be cautious, sir. But I do believe there might be a connection between that keep and the watery creature who plagues Mistress Olena's inn."

Hannon nodded and opened his mouth. But before he could speak, there was a knock at his door.

"Enter," he called.

The door opened to reveal several guards in fine livery. Hannon eyed them and frowned. "Well?" he said. "What is it?"

The guard in the lead stepped forward. "We are under orders of Lord Maladar to bring the stranger to their audience chamber at once," he said.

Anwyn felt his heart lurch.

"What has he done?" Captain Hannon asked.

"His Lordship has heard the visitor is a skilled harper and would hear him perform," the guard said, but there was something in his manner that told Anwyn this was not entirely true. "Will you come?" the guard asked, casting a challenging stare at Anwyn.

Clearly, I have no choice, Anwyn thought and slowly rose. "If it pleases his Lordship, I will gladly play for him. I am rather flattered he has heard of me at all."

The guard gestured for Anwyn to step into their ranks. He sighed and followed them out into the open chamber.

"Thank you, Captain Hannon," Anwyn called back.

The Captain did not reply.

EIGHT

They marched Anwyn out of the garrison, past the uncertain glances of Sergeant Throm and the other men, and back under the grand archway. He was taken towards the main gate of the keep that loomed over the arch. The portcullis had been raised and a contingency of guards now watched to make sure no unwanted visitors were allowed inside. Before he could be escorted through that opening, he spotted a familiar blue tunic and cloak coming out. Gordon was pocketing a small sack of coins and looking quite pleased. He stopped just under the arch and watched as Anwyn was brought towards the gate.

I might have known, Anwyn thought. Gordon stayed just long enough to smile, then turned and headed towards the stairs that would lead back into the Depths. Anwyn was whisked through the opening. Behind him, the ominous grate of the portcullis lowering once more shivered him to his bones.

I may have to use my gate song to leave this place.

:There is that possibility, Glynnanis hummed in his head. *:Because I sense something magical in this keep. Someone here may be a mage...*

Lords and Ladies! Anwyn fought hard not to frown.

He was herded up stairs and into a grand foray where tapestries of red and gold decorated the walls. The Lord of Stonegorge clearly had wealth, for everywhere, Anwyn saw fine furnishing and servants dressed in elaborate clothes and gilded carvings. But as he passed closer, he was aware of the frayed edges and the scent of old cloth and nicks in the gilt. Plus the servants wore tired expressions, and some of them looked terribly uncomfortable. Perhaps the trappings were not as fancy as they appeared?

Their little parade stopped before a set of mahogany doors that looked a little warped. Indeed, as the lead guard took hold of the handles, he was forced to give a firm tug to get them open. Anwyn took a deep breath.

There was moisture here. Perhaps not as heavy as in the Depths, but is presence scented the air and dampened the walls. Odd, for this high up, he would not have thought that possible, but a glance towards the windows at the far end of the corridor in which he stood revealed a heavy cloud hovering and leaving its kiss of moisture on the panes.

He would have asked Glynnanis, but he heard the leader of the guard party speaking.

"My Lord, my Lady, the harper from the Depths has been brought for your inspection."

Inspection?

"Bring him in," a man said wearily, "though I do not see why we have to do this..."

"Because strangers who questions our ways should always be brought in for inspection," a woman hissed as though trying to keep her voice low. "He could be an enemy."

"We have no..."

"Of course, we have enemies," she insisted. "He could be a spy from a foreign land! Or a thief come to steal what precious things we have."

"Precious little," the man muttered more to himself, though Anwyn could not miss the dismay in the tone.

The guards pushed Anwyn on through the doors, leaving him no room to balk.

He looked around at the room in awe. It was a huge chamber with marble and mosaic tiles and tapestries. At one end of the chamber on a dais were two ornate chairs of red velvet and gilded wood and a table festooned with food. Behind the table and chairs stood a contingency of guards, and on those chairs sat the owners of the voices.

He was a portly man with a beard trimmed to a point and a curling mustache, all going to grey and clearly meant to make up for what he lacked on top of his head. His clothes were quite simple compared to his servants, for he wore a black doublet and trousers edged in red silk trim.

She was just his opposite in clothes, though not in shape. A woman of matronly figure and composure, she apparently believed in showing off the enormous plain of white flesh below her chin. How was it Anwyn's eldest brother Gaelyn once put it when they looked upon portly guests who came to Nymbaria Hold from time to time. :*A man could get his head caught in there and suffocate...*

Anwyn stifled the urge to giggle at the memory, especially when he heard Glynnanis' chiming laughter.

The lady's face was pleasant, except for the edge of cruelty to the set of her mouth. She had been coiffed and painted to look ages younger, but it did nothing to enhance her in Anwyn's opinion. Her clothes were mixed shades of green and gold, and appeared to be the latest fashion of which she was aware, and her jewelry—he saw ornamentation and trinkets dangling from her wrists and her ears. The only thing about her throat was a single chain, and on the end of it dangled what looked like a piece of pewter in the shape of an eye and inset with an emerald that glittered strangely. *There's magic in that*, he thought as he looked once again at her face. Her eyes, however, were the dull grey of lead ore, and as soon as they met his silver stare, he saw her painted brows run briefly into a thick line over her nose.

She knows what my eyes mean, he thought, and that knowledge gave him no ease.

"Lord Maladar, Lady Rena, this is the harper Baldomyre."

"I do hope he knows some good songs," Lord Maladar said almost childishly. "Lunch tastes so much better when there is good music, don't you agree, my lamb?"

Anwyn blinked. Then he let years of courtly training take their cue. He had entertained Highlords and Dukes and Empresses and Kings on down to the lowliest of kitchen help. Stepping forward, he executed a most gracious bow.

"My good lord, my most gracious lady, I am your humble servant," he said. "How may I serve you?"

"They say you have a most wonderful harp," Lord Maladar said, and licked the grease of chicken from his fingers. "May we see?"

"Why certainly," Anwyn said. There was no stool, so he seated himself on the floor and drew Glynnanis from the cerecloth sack. Raking fingers across the strings to test the tuning, he launched into a lovely straspey. Within moments, Lord Maladar had dropped his food to his trencher and clapped his hands with glee.

"Oh, he is quite good, my dear," he said and looked at his wife. "We should have him stay for supper as well."

Anwyn picked himself up. "My lord, I thank you for your gracious offer," he said.

Lady Rena clearly did not share her husband's sentiments. She narrowed her leaden eyes and took a deep breath. "What brings you here, Harper Baldomyre?" she asked.

"Besides my own two feet, my lady?" Anwyn said. "Wandering lust, if you will. I am a harper, and a minstrel by trade, so I take myself from place to place, sharing the songs I know and learning new ones in the bargain, and composing them myself. What brings me here to Stonegorge? Well, it is the only way across, is it not?"

"It is said that you went into the Depths to find rooms, and that while you were there, a man died," she said.

"Yes, it was tragic," Anwyn agreed carefully. "He apparently drowned."

"And why did you think it necessary to speak to the captain of the garrison?"

Anwyn hesitated then sighed. "It is true I spoke to him, as I was curious about the marvelous stones that were used to shore up the walls of the Depths. I was told you were the one who discovered the source of that stone, and it was so beautiful, I was curious to know if there was more to be found at the source."

She frowned. "The source is none of your affair," she said.

"Oh, we found it at an old abandoned keep on the headwaters," Lord Maladar blurted almost simultaneously. "My wife knew of the place..."

The glance she threw Lord Maladar would have frozen a flame. But he didn't seem to notice.

"In fact, I dare say there is plenty more where that came from," Lord Maladar added.

"Tell me about this keep, my lord?" Anwyn asked.

"Ah, well, when I was a lad, it was said to have belonged to a witch woman," Lord Maladar said. His wife rolled her eyes. "But of course, she is dead and long gone now. So we took the stones."

"And why are you so interested in these stones?" Lady Rena interrupted.

"I am interested in anything that might make a good song," Anwyn replied and nodded courteously. "Indeed, I have plans of writing about the marvels of this place as well. Your bridge is most fascinating."

"Indeed," Lord Maladar said. "That would be wonderful indeed. To have a song about our bridge and our city. What would you call it?"

"The City Under the Bridge, of course," Anwyn said.

"Yes, that would be delightful."

"Really, my lord, we don't need a song about our city being bandied about," Lady Rena said.

"But of course we do," Lord Maladar retorted. "I've always wanted a song, and I shall have one. You will come back and sing it for us when it is finished, will you not?" He looked at Anwyn as he said that. "You know this bridge has stood for many generations. Which is why we needed the stone—to keep it from falling down."

"A noble gesture, my lord," Anwyn agreed. "But even now, from what I have seen in the Depths, I fear you will soon need more stone."

Lord Maladar sighed and leaned back in his chair. "Yes, you are right," he said. "It's the river, you know." He waved a pudgy hand towards the vista of the water and the distant mountains. "Some times it becomes a fury, and wears away the stone. This bridge has stood ten lifetimes of man, so one should not be surprised to find nature has taken its course. And rivers do rise..."

"Rivers deepen, my lord. Water cuts away stone like a knife and makes gorges deeper," Lady Rena said in a bored manner. "And anyway, if the rats who dwell in the Depths are so eager to stay dry, let them move to the upper levels and work for their betters to earn their keep."

"And where would be put them, my precious?" Lord Maladar asked. "That is why I tried to make the Depths stronger as I did. So those who dwell there could bloody well stay there. If we start cramming them into the middle arches, then Lower Stonegorge will become too heavy with the population. The foundations will be at an even greater risk."

"But if they were to move out of the Depths, we could turn it into a solid mass of stone with arches for the water to pass under, and we could shore up Stonegorge even better," she said with a visible pout. "And anyway, there are too many people here as it is, and if you would just tax them properly, we could have a better bridge. But no, you insist on being generous. I say the reason they are having troubles is there are just too many of them living down there, and they must be moved out if we are to save Stonegorge and its economy. If they don't like it, they can leave."

And I bet that is exactly what you would like for them to do, Anwyn thought.

"To displace people from their homes is wrong!" Lord Maladar retorted fiercely. "I shall not hear of it! No, we merely add more stone— take more from the keep and widen the foundations if we must, but we will not drive them out of their homes. It would not be fair to those who live in the Depths. Would you not agree with that, Master Anwyn?"

"Of course, my lord," Anwyn said and bowed again. "Now if you will excuse me, I do need to be on my way."

"You won't stay for supper then?" Lord Maladar asked in a disappointed manner. "We shall miss your good music...won't we, my precious?"

"Perhaps on my return," Anwyn said. "When I have finished my song about Stonegorge."

"Well, if you must leave, then, be off with you," Lord Maladar said. "Thank you for stopping in."

Anwyn tried not to laugh at the look of rage Lady Rena fought to keep hidden. It was clear to him she was not pleased to have her authority undermined by the man who ruled over her.

Smiling, Anwyn turned and started out of the hall. To his relief, no one stopped him from leaving. But until he passed through the doors, he could feel Lady Rena's eyes stabbing him in the back.

NINE

While Anwyn felt bad he did not go back to the Depths and give Olena a proper farewell, he did not want to risk having Lady Rena send the guards stop him. Clearly, she would have done so just for spite. So he left the keep and headed for the far end of the bridge. Digging out his token, he presented it the guards there. They bid him farewell, urged him to come again, and left him to the road.

On this side of the river gorge, the road climbed to the very top of the cliffs. For such a long ways, Anwyn was able to see much of Stonegorge when he looked back. But at last, the river took a turn, and so did the road, and the cliffs of stone edged in a verdant and umber forest blocked his view.

His road split as well, dividing and sending part of it ambling into the trees. The rest continued to course the river's edge.

"So, we follow the river to the headwater, then," Anwyn said aloud.

:*Water, water, water—what it is with you and water?* Glynnanis scolded.

"I'm not interested in the water," Anwyn retorted. "I am interested in the keep."

:*Waste of time, I think,* the harp retorted. :*If the mage is dead, what purpose is there in bothering to visit her keep and...*

"You know as well as I that there has to be some sort of connection," Anwyn said. "That creature has to be a water wraith."

:*Of course, there is, but that's no reason to waste time looking at a deserted keep!* Glynnanis said. :*It isn't always wise to meddle in the affairs of strange mages—especially dead ones.*

"But you're the one who is always telling me I should be more curious about magic," Anwyn said.

:*Not when there is water involved.*

Anwyn shook his head.

At midday, he stopped and sat on a log overlooking the gorge as he devoured the last bit of cheese and bread in his satchel. Sadly, he had forgotten to ask Mistress Olena for food for the road. His next meal—assuming he was still in the wild—would have to consist of what he could forage. Or what he could conjure from Rhystar's stores with his Song of Feasting.

I wonder what Rhystar is doing now? Is it still night where he is? Is he asleep? Granted neither night nor day mattered to the master of Far Reach—like all mages, he had made his sacrifice for the power, depriving him of one of the five senses in exchange for the power. And while he had a means of disguising the handicap, there were times Anwyn worried. He had gated back to Far Reach a few times since he began his travels through Lamboria, and there were times he feared Rhystar would not be there. Rhystar was ancient, even by Thuathyn standards, and though he seemed youthful at times, it was clear some days he was not as strong as others. *What if I go back and he is gone?*

He owed much to Rhystar, and the thought of losing the old mage, though inevitable, was always going to be his worst fear. It was Rhystar who taught Anwyn to be himself, and to accept himself as he was.

:*You could know these things if you made your sacrifice*, Glynnanis said.

Anwyn sighed and rose from the log, shaking his head as he picked up his satchel and the cerecloth sack then slung them over his shoulder again. "I will not give up one of my senses to be a prisoner of the magic," he said.

:*That is what you always say*, the harp replied.

"Then why do you bother to ask?" Anwyn said as he pushed the remorseful thoughts aside and headed on.

Perhaps a league had gone under his feet, and the afternoon sun started to drift towards the horizon. The gorge, he noticed, was growing much narrower, less than half the width it was before. The river was wilder, dashing over sharp rocks, cascading down faces of stone in small white waterfalls. The fury that it had in passing under Stonegorge seemed greater here, but Anwyn knew it was because the water was channeled tighter and dropping from heights.

The sun had barely touched the top of the trees when Anwyn stopped. Before him, he saw a great waterfall, water spurting out of a cave in the rocks where the sides of the gorge finally narrowed and met. And wedged in above this gush of water stood the remains of a keep. Box-shaped, with a lone circular tower, it clung decrepitly to the landscape on which it had been built, as though someone had haphazardly crammed it into the narrow point where the gorge ended and then piled on more structure. But even from the road, he could see the structure had fallen on hard times. The stones of its high walls had been torn away, leaving great gaping holes.

"One could march an army through those broken walls," Anwyn muttered.

:*It looks like someone did*, Glynnanis agreed.

Shifting his sacks for comfort, Anwyn started on toward the keep. Dark would soon fall, and he could already hear the distant howls of wolves echoing through the forest. The sun was even lower by the time he reached what had once been a great stone gate and stepped into a yard gone to ruin. The orchard within looked neglected. Brambles were everywhere, leaving not much of a path through what must have once been a fine garden.

He stopped and looked up at the tower once more. No light glittered from the single black eye of a window that stared towards the river.

"Looks to me like no one lives here," he said.

:*So maybe we should leave?* Glynnanis suggested. :*I bet there are holes in the roof that let rain in.*

"Do you actually sense anything evil here?" Anwyn asked.

:*Well, no*, the harp said hesitantly. :*But I do sense old magic, and that seems as good a reason as any to leave.*

"Magic or not, we need shelter for the night, and this is as good as any," Anwyn said.

:*Where have I heard that before?* the harp said with a sniff.

Anwyn frowned and continued on his way. The doors of the keep were large wooden things, one of which dangled from a single hinge. Cautiously, he stepped into grey shadows where spiders were taking over cracks and crevices and ivy crawled across the floor. A short tunnel opened out into what had once been a grand hall. Shafts of pale light in the gloaming filtered through high windows. He could hear doves in the rafters.

:*I don't like the look of this*, Glynnanis said.

"You never like the look of anything," Anwyn whispered, and his voice echoed eerily through the gloom. His eyes were adjusting, and he could make out old tapestries torn from their moorings and crumpled on the floor, furniture smashed into firewood. The fire pit sat cold; though he had the impression from the odors of wood smoke someone had tried to start a fire there not long ago.

Across from him, he could see stairs, and on the ledge above, he made out what must have been the door to the tower.

He took a deep breath and called, "Hello?"

No one answered. Frowning, Anwyn advanced a few more steps. He was looking up at the tatters of tapestries when his feet found an uneven bit of flagstone. Anwyn stumbled and as he fought for balance, he hit a small stool sitting near the fire pit and sent it crashing over.

Frantic wings clattered in the rafters above. His clumsiness had startled the doves, and he barely dodged the excrement that rained down on him in from their fright. He dashed over towards the nearest niche, shaking his head in disgust.

:*Well, that was clever*, Glynnanis mused. :*Whoever is here will know you have come for certain now.*

It was on the tip of Anwyn's tongue to tell the harp to go jump in the river when he heard the whine of a wooden door on rusty hinges. Anwyn froze in place, letting the shadows of the niche hide him. Rasping breaths followed the grating.

And then an old woman said, "Who's there?"

Anwyn frowned. Cautiously, he worked his way closer to the edge, peering around the rough stones.

She stood no higher than his shoulder, and her frazzled white hair hung in clouds where it escaped her attempts to braid it. Wizen of frame, she clutched worn robes about her that had seen better days and leaned on a staff of grey wood. Her face held a winsome beauty in spite of the masses of wrinkles, and her eyes—they were the opaque silver of a mage who had sacrificed their sight.

"Who is there?" she repeated, and her voice hinted of fear. One hand fluttered out as though trying to keep track of the wall. She took a step to one side, cocking her head back and forth like a bird. "Tarena? Rilla? Oh, please, is someone there?"

Perhaps it was the weariness and the fear. Anwyn sighed as guilt rushed him in waves.

"I am sorry, madam, I did not mean to frighten you," he said as he stepped out of the niche.

"Who are you?" she whimpered, clutching the staff more firmly as though she would defend herself—or try. "Stay back! I've nothing left to steal!"

"My name is Anwyn Baldomyre, and I am a harper and a minstrel by trade. And I have not come to steal from you, but to seek your council."

"Come closer. Let me touch you so I might know you speak true."

Anwyn cautiously stepped across the flagstones and climbed the stairs to the upper level, approaching the base of the tower and the now open door. He stopped in front of her. "I am here," he said, noticing how she searched back and forth.

She is blind, he thought.

Her hand reached hesitantly, and finding his chest, it worked upwards until she touched his face.

"No armor," she said. "And no weapon, so you are not a soldier, but you could be a thief. Say your name again."

Her flesh felt cold as her fingers wandered his features. Anwyn sighed and said, "Anwyn Baldomyre. And I am no thief. I am the son of a gamekeeper who would never have tolerated any such behavior from any of my siblings."

She took a deep breath. "Your accent is not Lamborian. Your aura says you are Thuathyn."

"That I am," he said and smiled.

"You are a handsome one," she said and her hand dropped. "I wish I could see your face. Alas, I cannot find my other eye."

"I am sorry," he repeated. "I truly did not mean to frighten you. I was seeking shelter for the night and information as well. I was in Stonegorge last night, and I was told about this place, but they seemed to believe the owner was dead and this keep deserted."

"I might as well be as far as they are concerned," she said. "They have stolen from me without fear, and I was unable to stop them, so I fear I have little of value left other than my life. I would offer you a place by the fire, but I cannot seem to light it anymore..."

Her words trailed off.

"I will light a fire for you," Anwyn said.

:*You're not going to use...* Glynnanis began, and the old woman gasped.

"You are not alone," she said, and the panic in her voice returned. "Who else is here? You came from Stonegorge? You have come to rob me, haven't you?"

"No, no," Anwyn said. "I...that was my harp."

"Your harp?" She frowned in confusion. "Your harp speaks? Are you—a mage as well as Thuathyn?"

"No, I have not made the sacrifice," Anwyn said.

"Is that why you've come? Seeking a master to teach you?"

"No," Anwyn said and smiled, even though he knew she could not see him do so. "I travel the world seeking adventure and songs. I am a friend of Rhystar of Far Reach, and my harp is Glynnanis, whom he made years ago and..."

"Rhystar of Far Reach?" Awe stretched her mouth into a smile. "I knew him once. You mean to say he is still alive?"

"Yes," Anwyn said.

"Oh, I do wonder if he would remember Larana of High Gorge?"

"I am sorry, but I have never heard him mention that name," Anwyn said.

Larana shook her head. "It does not matter. If you have not come to learn or to steal from me, then why are you here?"

"Because I need to talk to you about the creature that plagues Stonegorge with watery death," Anwyn said.

Her eyes narrowed. "You know what it is, don't you?"

"I think I do," Anwyn said. "But I wanted to be certain."

"Then come with me and light me a fire in my personal hearth," she said in a more confident voice. "The birds make staying down here now too risky, and beside, I have not had a good cup of tea in several moons now. Sorry, but I have little more to offer."

"I think I can change that," Anwyn said.

She turned, trying to find the door.

"Here, allow me," he said and took her hand, offering his arm.

She smiled as he helped her find the door and entered the tower with her.

TEN

The tower chamber displayed the random clutter Anwyn had come to associate with all who practiced magic, but this room showed signs of having been ransacked in some fashion. Larana gestured randomly about and spoke of chairs, and all Anwyn could find was one with a worn cushion. No matter, he told himself. He seated the old woman there and proceeded to clear debris from the grate of her small hearth and replace it with wood from broken furniture that looked like it had been purposely smashed.

Once the wood was set in the grate, Anwyn took a deep breath and sang his Song of Fire. Flames popped and crackled about the logs.

"Oh, that feels nice," Larana said. "There should still be tea in the cupboard."

"In a moment," Anwyn said, and once more, he closed his eyes. Reaching for the notes of his Song of Feasting, he sang it, concentrating on Rhystar's stores. Within moments, there was bread and cheese and fruit and a shank of lamb, and a jug of wine, and the odors that filled the air made his own mouth water in anticipation.

Larana giggled like a girl and clapped her hands. "I smell cheese!"

Anwyn broke her off a bit from the wedge and put it in her hands. She nibbled on it as he fetched a kettle and found two cups left unbroken by whatever tragedy had taken place. Water was no problem. He discovered a small rill coming in through a hole in the wall and vanishing through another in the floor, and was able to get clean water.

"Impressive, isn't it," Larana said. "Rilla made that for me. So I would not have to go down to the well for water."

"Who is Rilla?" Anwyn asked as he set the kettle on to boil.

Larana sighed. "She is a water wraith, and she is gone. Is there more cheese?"

Anwyn sorted out a pear, broke off more cheese and some bread and a bit of meat and put them on a wooden platter, and then handed them to Larana. She smiled as she felt of her meal, and then began to eat her fill. And once the water was boiling, Anwyn made the tea and handed her a cup. She looked so delighted.

"You make tea as well as Rilla did," she finally said as she finished her meal.

"Thank you," Anwyn replied. "There's plenty more, enough to see you for a few days, at least."

Her smile faded just slightly. "Yes, I thank you for that. And now, since you have been kind enough to feed me and not steal from me, I shall tell you whatever you want to know."

"Then start by telling me what happened here," he said.

Larana sighed. "It is hard to say when it all began. I came here as a young girl, apprenticed to the former master of this keep, and when he died, he left me but a few things—this keep, his knowledge, Rilla's heart stone and his child growing in me. I soon gave birth to his daughter with Rilla attending me.

"In those days, I thought we were happy, but I was soon to learn the child I had spawned was possessed with a most unnatural greed. Tarena coveted power and possessions in her heart. She was always a needy child, and I tried hard to teach her frugal ways, but she always wanted more than was her due. I saw her eyes were lead-colored and thought perhaps it was the magic in her that made her this way. I assumed she would be my apprentice when she was old enough to come into her power and make her sacrifice.

"But she was not satisfied to learn what I had to teach. She would torment Rilla and insist that if the wraith would assist her, she would set her free. But I think even Rilla could see into Tarena's heart and know this was not true. She told me what Tarena was plotting...

"I will admit I was angry, and I swore that until Tarena learned kindness, she would never have what I possessed. That did not set well with her, and when she was old enough, she decided she no longer wanted to live here, so she went out on her own."

Larana stopped and sighed, and then took a sip of her tea.

"Do you know where she went?" Anwyn asked.

"Of course, I know," Larana said. "Rilla often plays in the river. I let her run up and down it because I knew it made her happy to do so, and one day, she came to me and told me she had found Tarena. She said my daughter had taken up residence downriver in the city of Stonegorge, and she had managed to get herself wed to the master of that place. She said Tarena wore finery like a badge and had grown quite stout, and ill-used any who stood against her."

"So Tarena is Lady Rena of Stonegorge," Anwyn said.

"Is that what she calls herself?" Larana snorted.

"Yes," Anwyn said. "She is married to the Lord of Stonegorge. Now her greed is tearing people there apart. But worse than that, I think I know what happened to Rilla, for the people who live in the Depths are plagued by a water wraith they call the Water Lady."

"This cannot be. Rilla would never harm anyone unless provoked. Tarena must have done something to make the water wraith angry."

"She trapped Rilla's stone in one of the columns that supports the bridge of Stonegorge," Anwyn said. "Rilla is tearing out the very foundations trying to reclaim it."

"But why would Tarena want Rilla to destroy the bridge?"

"Not the whole bridge, I gather, but the homes of those too poor to pay the high tariffs she tried to inflict on them so she can have all her finery. Rilla has flooded the lowermost cellars. And she has killed, though if what you say is true, she may do so only if those she kills get in her way as she seeks her heart stone."

Larana took a deep breath. "This is terrible," she said. "Would that I could find my pendant and come to Stonegorge, I would help Rilla reclaim her stone and escape."

Anwyn glanced at his harp. Glynnanis angled its head in response.

"There is a way," he said softly. "But it could be dangerous for us both."

"I have seen many years and many things," Larana said. "Danger does not frighten me."

"I am certain Lady Rena has your pendant," Anwyn said. "She wore a stone like an emerald eye about her neck. But I do not think she has made the sacrifice to set her own power free."

"I need that pendant to see," Larana said.

"Then why don't I take you back to Stonegorge and we will see about wresting this pendant from her and setting Rilla free."

"You would do that for me?" Larana asked.

"Shelter me tonight," Anwyn said. "Tomorrow morning early we will go to Stonegorge by way of my Gate Song. For I know where we can find allies to assist us."

"We shall do it," Larana said. "Sleep where you wish."

"Thank you," he said.

:I hope you know what you are doing, Glynnanis said. *:Taking us back to*

Stonegorge by magical means could be dangerous. You know how superstitious these Lamborians are when it comes to magic...

Larana looked straight at the harp and smiled. "Does it always sound so defensible?"

Anwyn grinned. "Worse at times," he said.

:*That's right, pick on me*, Glynnanis said.

"Shall I pick on your strings instead?" Anwyn asked.

:*I suppose*, the harp replied in a grumpy voice.

Anwyn laughed as he took up the harp and began to play.

ELEVEN

Anwyn was very pleased with his playing that night. Larana praised him even as she dozed off in her chair. He gently helped her to her bed, covered her with blankets and left her there, then settled himself before the fire on a rug to sleep.

Dawn came stretching amber and coral fingers through the slit windows. His fire had turned to coals, so he coaxed them back to life with wood and his own breath rather than waste magic. By the time he had water boiling for more tea, Larana had awakened.

"Good morning, lady," Anwyn said.

She sat up and blinked owlishly as though uncertain at first why she was hearing his voice. But then she asked, "Do I smell tea?"

"Indeed," Anwyn said as he swilled water into the delicate leaves and swirled them in the pot. "Would you like honey?"

"Oh, yes, please," she said.

He added a bit of honey into the mix, and then took a cup to Larana, carefully folding her hands around the warm mug. She blew on it and sipped it cautiously at first, then with enthusiasm.

At length, they had warmed themselves with tea and fed on soft bread and fruit Larana told Anwyn where to find her cloak. He bundled her into it, then helped her down the spiral of stairs to the main room.

Sunlight now filtered through the windows. Anwyn could smell the water from the falls permeating the air. He had told Larana what he would be doing, so she stood patiently grasping his arm while he closed his eyes and took a deep breath and reached inside himself for the notes of his Gate Song. He concentrated on the room at the inn where he had spent the night and prayed as he let his song spill forth that Mistress Olena had not rented the room to another. As he sang, he drew Larana close and stepped into the dark, airless void. He had instructed her not to let go, and she obeyed as he walked through the rift into a chamber where light barely crept through the curtained windows. He had even managed to land even instead of dropping from heights as he so often did when he did not have time to concentrate as well.

"Are we there?" Larana asked.

Anwyn looked around. No one was in the chamber. "Yes, we are here, and if you will sit here for a moment, I will make our presence known to our hostess."

He led Larana to the chair and seated her there, then softly, he stepped over to the door. Barely opening it, he peered out into the hall. He could hear the sound of voices raised in a heated argument.

"Is it not safe for you to remain here, Olena," a man barked. *Captain Hannon*, Anwyn thought. "Soon enough, this whole level will be flooded," Hannon said.

"I will not leave!" Olena said. "It is just another one of her tricks! Warning us of the danger, indeed. The only real danger to Stonegorge is that woman who tries to force us out of our homes."

"The danger of flooding is quite real," Hannon said. "The water level has risen three markers just since last night, and it shows no sign of letting up. Another marker and your floors will be flooded. Two more and the river will drag you out of this place."

"And just where am I supposed to go?" Olena asked.

"You could come and live with me," Hannon said. "You could consent to be my wife."

"And give up my inn? Never!"

The captain heaved a tumultuous sigh. "Olena, I love you."

"Then stop trying to make me leave," she said.

Anwyn sighed and glanced back at Larana. *We cannot hide here*, he thought.

He opened the door and boldly stepped into the hall.

Olena and Hannon stood just inside the hall near the door of the common room. At the sight of the harper, Hannon reached for his sword, and Olena gasped and turned. Seeing Anwyn, her expression shifted from fright to puzzlement.

"Master Anwyn," she said. "I thought you had left us..."

"I did," Anwyn said, "but I brought someone back with me who may be able to help us with the Water Lady."

He stepped back and gestured into the room. Still puzzled, Olena walked over to the door. Captain Hannon followed her, his eyes full of suspicion. Anwyn moved back into the room so they could enter.

"Mistress Olena, Captain Hannon, this is Larana of High Gorge."

Larana bowed her head in a regal manner.

"Welcome to the Waterhouse Inn," Olena said. "But I am not certain I understand—how did you get here?"

"Magic, of course," Larana said as though it were common knowledge.

Olena looked at Anwyn.

"I am sorry. I should have told you," he said. "I am one born with magic's gift—you Lamborians call us *witch folk*, I believe. Mistress Larana is also a mage. And she is Lady Rena's mother..."

"What?" Hannon looked angry. "You mean to say you are one of those witches who have plagued us from time to time? How dare you come here with your accusations and..."

Olena stepped in between Anwyn and Hannon. "Hannon, be at peace." She looked into Anwyn's eyes as she spoke. "My brother was a mage as you well know."

Hannon drew himself up and stepped back.

"He defied Lady Rena on several matters, and I do once remember him saying she had the mark of a mage on her. And it was not long after that the rivers flooded and he lost his life saving another. There are times I have wondered if Lady Rena had planned his death, for once he was gone, she became more serious in her desire to get us out of the Depths."

"I am sorry to hear my daughter has caused so much ill in this place," Larana said softly. "I will do what I can to make amends, but first, I must have my pendant restored to me, for with it I will be able to find the heart stone of the water wraith that now plagues you."

"So where is this pendant?" Olena asked.

"Lady Rena wears it," Anwyn replied. "I saw it when I was taken into the palace. It has a green stone set in pewter shaped like an eye"

"And just how do you propose we take it from Lady Rena?" Hannon asked gruffly. "For I have seen this pendant of which you speak. Lady Rena never takes it off. She once told his lordship it was a memento of her childhood when he complained it did not match her other jewels."

"I have a plan, but I need to get into the palace," Anwyn said. "And we must wait until tomorrow, because I have already used my Gate Song and must sleep before I can use it again..."

"Mistress Olena?"

Anwyn froze as a small head popped around the corner of the open doorway. It was the potboy Linden who stood there with his eyes round with uncertainty.

"What is it, Linden?" Olena asked. "Have you been spying on us?"

"No, Mistress," the boy sputtered uneasily. "But we've got business. Some of the watch are here looking for a meal, and you know I can't fix a decent pot o' soup."

The watch? Anwyn thought.

"Tell them I will have soup ready shortly," she said, shooing him away. She turned back to the others. "I am sorry, but business is business. Come on out and bring Mistress Larana, and I'll fix some tea and honey bread for us to share. Once everything settles down, we can talk more about this plan."

Anwyn nodded. He offered Larana his arm, helping her out of the chair and leading her towards the door.

The common room was already a clamor of impatient voices demanding food. As Anwyn stepped into the chamber and led Larana to a booth, he glanced over the bevy of familiar uniforms.

And ducked his head when he realized Gordon was among them.

Lords and Ladies! he thought as he settled down with his back to the others. *I hope he didn't see me.*

He sat down and waited for Olena to deal with her customers.

TWELVE

The watchmen seemed to stay forever, but finally, they drifted out in pairs, only to be replaced by a few of the local fisher folk. Anwyn kept watching to make certain Gordon was gone before he dared to stand up and look around at all. Larana enjoyed her tea and honey bread, chattering like a delighted child over the delicate flavor of each.

At length, Hannon and Olena were back to join them in the booth.

"It is safe to talk now," Olena said. "But we must stay out here in case more customers come in."

Anwyn nodded. Just as long as the watch had left, he thought it would be fine.

"So you said you had a plan," Olena said.

"I have a song—a sleep song," Anwyn said. "It's one of the spells I can work. If we can get into the palace, I can sing it and put Lady Rena and all around her to sleep. And while I sing it, we can remove the pendant from her neck and bring it back here to Larana."

"You would have me stay here?" Larana asked.

"It would be better if there were less of us to be caught," Anwyn said. He glanced at Hannon who was frowning. "Is there a way in?"

Hannon sighed. "There is a passage from the garrison—and emergency route of escape for those who live in the palace. But it only goes as far as the kitchen quarters. Apparently, someone bricked up the rest of the passage ages ago to strengthen a pillar that was supporting one corner of the palace." He paused, looking thoughtful before he spoke again. "In fact, it seems to me that it was Lady Rena's idea…"

"Sounds like she was afraid someone would find a way in," Larana said. "My daughter knows well there are many who would seek to steal what she has stolen from me."

"Just as you would steal it from her?" the captain asked.

"I am not stealing," Larana said testily. "I am reclaiming what is mine by right. My daughter has stolen my power and my sight"

Hannon rolled his eyes and looked at Anwyn again. "So you would have me lead you into the palace by a secret way, allow you to enchant my lady and steal her trinket, and then return you here?"

"That is the gist of it," Anwyn said.

"Sounds like a foolish plan," Hannon muttered.

"It is the only one I have," Anwyn said. "If you can think of another way of taking the pendant from her, by all means, enlighten us."

Hannon frowned. "Well, no. I just wanted to be certain this was all you wanted to do."

Now Olena rolled her eyes then frowned towards the door. Anwyn was tempted to turn and see what had her attention, but she looked back at him instead. "It is a sound plan, and I would suggest waiting until night falls to enact upon it. And as for you, Hannon, if you love me as much as you claim, you will help him to do this and stop being so miserably pessimistic."

Hannon sighed. "Of course, I love you. But what if he is caught? What if I am caught? The Lady Rena will not be kind. She will have us both thrown from the highest walls of Stonegorge."

"I do not wish that to happen," Anwyn said. "Which is why it would be better to go in the shadow time. Everyone will be too tired to care about a couple of guards wandering in and out."

Hannon smiled. "So you propose to disguise yourself?" he said.

"And to leave my harp here," Anwyn said, and immediately felt a twinge of regret.

:*Fine, leave me here where it is wet*, Glynnanis said.

"You poor thing, don't fret so," Larana said, and she reached over and tried to find the harp as though to pet it. "I will look after you and keep you dry."

Anwyn bit his lip when he heard Glynnanis snort derisively. Besides, Olena and Hannon were staring at Larana as though she had lost all her wits.

But then Olena glanced back to the door once more. "Linden, go see what that great oaf wants," she said.

The potboy put down the tankard he was drying out and rushed towards the door.

"What else will you need?" Hannon asked.

"I will need to sleep in order to restore my gate spell song, for I fear that may be the only way we can escape should our plan fail," Anwyn said. "If that is not a problem, Mistress Olena, I shall need a room" he swiftly added.

"Not at all," she said. "You can use the room you had before.

I'll put Mistress Larana up in the one next to you so she can rest as well."

"How much?" Anwyn asked.

"Oh, there is no need for payment," Olena said. "If what you are planning helps to free Stonegorge from Lady Rena's tyranny then so be it."

"You are too generous," Anwyn said.

"Indeed," Hannon said with a sneer.

"Behave yourself, my love," Olena said, "Or I will make you sleep with in the cellar."

"Your cellars are flooded," he protested, putting a hand over his heart in mock affront.

"The top steps are still dry," she insisted.

At that moment, Linden slipped back in, casting a furtive glance at them as he rushed for the bar.

"So what did Gordon want, boy?" Olena said.

Linden stopped, and Anwyn felt his own heart thump. Gordon had been at the door? Had he seen Anwyn?

"He wanted a pot of ale, Mistress," Linden replied. "Said he needed it to warm him on his watch."

"Did he offer to pay?" she asked.

"No, Mistress," Linden said.

"So what did you tell him?" she asked.

Linden grinned in a lopsided manner, though Anwyn could not help but notice that the corner of the boy's mouth quivered. "I told him to go sod himself, Mistress, as we didn't do no charity as long as there was a tariff bleeding us dry…"

"Good lad," Olena said. "You are learning."

Linden smiled even more and rushed towards the bar.

THIRTEEN

With Larana safely ensconced in the next room, Anwyn was able to fall asleep for a time. He dreamed of water, of floating in it, clutching Glynnanis to his chest. Of riding water rapidly down a deep gorge and of passing under a bridge whose stone span was crumbling and tumbling into the river around him. As he stared up at the stone, he sensed a bright spark of magic buried in its depths, so close he could almost reach out and touch it with his fingers.

But as he reached to touch it, to snatch it out of the stone, a hand snagged his wrist and a face suddenly loomed, a large face full of rage. Under the quivering chins, he spied an eye embedded in the throat, and he reached for that as well. But the hand held his at bay, and the woman started to scream, and as she screamed, the stones of the bridge tumbled and fell, splashing into the water around him, churning it into a white flood and threatening to sink him beneath the choppy surface. He tried to break free, but she would not let go. Her hand turned into water, her face thinned, and he saw the translucent woman who had stood at the window. Smiling, she leaned down to kiss him, and as her lips claimed his, she drove water deep into his lungs.

Anwyn sat us suddenly in the bed, sputtering and gasping for air. A moist thickness prevailed with the shadows. His gaze darted furtively about, and then he remembered where he was.

:*Dreaming, are we?* Glynnanis asked.

Anwyn merely nodded.

:*Are you going to be all right?* the harp sang.

"I'll be fine," Anwyn muttered. "I just dreamed the wraith was drowning me."

He glanced at the curtained window. No light seeped through the cracks. Rising from the bed, he crossed the chamber and pushed one of the old drapes aside.

Moonlight was playing on the white water that rushed from beneath the bridge. It turned the river into a tumble of pearls. Anwyn took a deep breath, drinking in the beauty, wondering if he could compose a song, when he heard a light rapping on the door.

"Who is it?" he asked.

"Hannon," a voice replied.

Anwyn sighed and pulled away from the window, opening the door. The old guardsman stood there, swathed in dark clothing, a cloak over his arm.

"It is nearing the dark hour," he said. "Olena is making us tea to keep us alert."

"Alert would be good," Anwyn agreed as he half stumbled out of the chamber.

:*Wait, are you going to leave me here alone?* Glynnanis protested.

I will return, Anwyn thought and followed Hannon into the common room where Olena was indeed preparing a tea. Larana was there as well, sipping from one of the cups. The rest of the inn was silent, except for the snores.

I must have slept a long time, Anwyn thought. Good, that meant he would have his gate spell song and all the rest at his disposal.

He took a place at the table, and Olena handed him tea and some white cheese and bread.

"You need food," she said.

Anwyn nodded and ate his fill, as did Hannon. They said nothing, wanting the silence in order not to awaken any of the other guests.

In a short time, Hannon and Anwyn were slipping out of the inn, staring at the darkness. Hannon had arranged passage to the top on one of the baskets.

"I hope you know this is costing several pence," he said. "The baskets do not normally operate after dark, except by special order."

"Doesn't the watch use them?" Anwyn asked as he held the seat and felt the basket ascending.

Hannon frowned, but he nodded. "Yes, they are the only ones who can order the baskets at any time. But they must have a good reason besides wanting to desert their posts and rise to a better class of ale than they can get in the Depths. Why do you ask?"

Anwyn shrugged. "I just wondered."

Hannon said nothing. He stared out of the small aperture that served as a window. Anwyn wrapped his cloak tighter. The night wind whistled through the basket, catching tendrils of Anwyn's coppery hair and stinging his eyes. He felt just a bit out of sorts at the moment, not having his harp in hand. And it occurred to him Glynnanis might have been useful after all, if only for companionship.

Why am I doing this?

Because he cared too much, he imagined. Olena was a good woman. Larana was clearly a good woman too. Hannon—well, he might be gruff and think Anwyn was bringing naught by trouble on their heads, but he was still a decent man.

I do this for them because they are good people and do not deserve the fate Lady Rena has chosen for them. To drive them out of their homes was wrong.

The basket lurched suddenly to the side. Anwyn felt his stomach heave, and was glad for the tea and bread and cheese. There was a dizzy moment followed by the jarring of a thump on solid ground. The basket door was unbound, and Hannon stepped out first. Anwyn followed, peering about at the night.

No sign of any watchman, at least.

"This way," Hannon said, and he crossed the cobbles to the stairs. They climbed to the top of Stonegorge's bridge, keeping to the shadows. The captain knew his path well. He walked straight into the garrison, nodding to the guards. Anwyn had been told to stay close and keep his head down as they passed, and to try and look a little tipsy. Not difficult since he still felt a little woozy from the ride.

"Captain?" a voice said as they reached the garrison gates. "You've been out rather late. And who is this?"

"A young recruit who strayed into the Depths," Hannon said.

"Do you want me to put him in the brig?" the guard asked, and Anwyn's heard skipped a few beats.

"No, no," Hannon said. "I shall deal with the matter myself. I am going to have to write him up before I send him to his bed to sleep off his ale. Carry on."

Anwyn wanted to look up and see if the guard believed them, but he dared not let them see his silver eyes. Hannon's hand seized his shoulder as though admonishing him and harshly shoved him through the garrison gates. Their rapid march did not stop until they had passed through the sleep quarters and entered Hannon's own office. Only then did he release Anwyn who staggered for balance.

"We won't have long," Hannon said. "If they think I am in here with you too long, they will wonder what sort of discipline I had in mind."

There was a hint of amusement in his words as he spoke. Anwyn arched an eyebrow then shook his head.

"Bolt the door, will you," Hannon said. "Quietly, of course."

Anwyn sighed and crossed over to the door, carefully sliding the bolt into place. By the time he turned back, Hannon had opened a small door behind one of the tapestries, and was holding the cloth aside.

"Well, come on," Hannon said. "We don't want to take all night, do we? Oh, and bring that small lantern off my desk."

And just who put you in charge? Anwyn wondered, but he hurried across the room, grabbing the lantern in passing, and stepped through the door.

FOURTEEN

The chamber was close, and the light of the lantern played over the stones. There was another opening across from the one Hannon now stepped through and shut in his wake. Through it, Anwyn could see stairs.

"Hope you're up for a bit of climbing," Hannon said.

"Do we have a choice?" Anwyn asked.

"Well, yes, we could give up this nonsense and go back and convince Olena it would be better for her to leave the Depths and marry me."

"So you really are in love with her," Anwyn said as he started up the circle of narrow stairs. Even here, there was dampness to the walls.

"With all my heart," Hannon said. "She is a good woman, and I would hate to see anything happen to her because of this venture of yours."

"I give you my word that nothing will happen to her," Anwyn said. "If I must use magic to bear her to safety, I will."

"I'll hold you to that," Hannon said. "Now save your breath for climbing."

Anwyn nodded and continued on. His light bounced off the moisture that slithered down the walls. He could smell water in the air, and the passage was thick with moisture. Under his feet, the stones looked well worn, making him wonder just how old Stonegorge was and whether this passage had served as more than a route of escape. All around, he could feel the closeness of the stone. And the vague hint of magic far below his feet pulsed.

"This is one of the support pillars, is it not?" Anwyn asked.

"Yes, but I told you that."

"Does it go all the way down to the Depths?"

"Why do you ask?"

"Curious, that's all," Anwyn said.

"Curiosity can spoil your wind on a climb like this," Hannon said. "But yes, I believe it does. It's one of the four great pillars built when Stonegorge was new, they say. Before it grew into the city it is today. At one time, these stairs descended all the way to the base, but over time, they were filled in to make them stronger. In fact, the ones below us are stuffed with the stones that came from that old keep."

"The same one Lady Rena tossed her stone into?"

Hannon frowned. "What are you suggesting?"

Only that I might know where the water wraith's heart stone lies, Anwyn thought. And if so, why was he bothering to climb to danger?

Because I promised Larana I would reclaim her pendant.

"What are you suggesting?" Hannon repeated.

Anwyn sighed. "Nothing. Nothing at all. I just wondered."

He stopped talking then, concentrating on the climb.

Which proved a valuable effort for even though they were only climbing the height of several floors, Anwyn felt his legs growing weary. *I would have to be strong to live here all the time*, he thought.

Not that Glynnanis would enjoy it.

He hoped the harp was okay. Larana said she would look after Glynnanis, but Anwyn had left the harp in the room in which he slept.

Then again, knowing how Glynnanis could carry on, it was probably for the better.

"Stop," Hannon suddenly whispered. "This is as high as we can go."

Anwyn froze. He raised the lantern, peering around the next turn and was greeted by the sight of stone blocking the passage.

"Where are we?" Anwyn said, and just a hint of dread crept into his voice. He saw no door—no means of entering the palace. Was this a trap? Had Hannon led him here for some more nefarious purpose? He turned a frightened look on the old guard, but Hannon was busy pressing various stones with his fingers.

"It has to be one of these," Hannon muttered.

It occurred to Anwyn he could smell baked bread and meats. And there was a visible crack in the wall through which the faintest hint of firelight exuded.

The stones suddenly parted, revealing the kitchen. Anwyn stepped back, startled. Hannon took the lead now and slipped through the gap. They were in a corner of the kitchen, just behind a massive fireplace— the source of the light. Hannon gestured for Anwyn to hold back as he slipped forward to investigate. From somewhere in the room, Anwyn could hear snores.

After a moment, Hannon motioned for Anwyn to follow. He stepped quietly through the gap in the wall, glancing about in uncertainty A large kitchen greeted him, and over by the fire, a woman in cook's aprons sprawled in a chair and snored.

Odd. Kitchens in great houses in Nymbaria were usually chaotic with activity whether it was day or night. There were guards to be fed at all hours, meals to prepare, and game to dress. Yet before Anwyn was a large empty space lit only by a fire. *This cannot be right*, Anwyn thought.

Hannon had already made his way across the floor to the entrance on the far end. He jerked his hand in a 'come quickly' motion. Anwyn took one look at the cook and followed, his unease growing. Only a cook? Where were the potboys and scullery maids and assistant cooks? Had Lady Rena drained the coffers to the point they could not afford servants?

At the door, Hannon crouched and looked into the hall. Anwyn leaned so he could look as well and saw no guards. He shook his head. There had been many guards when he was brought before the Lord and Lady of Stonegorge. Surely they didn't all have the night off. He leaned close to Hannon and whispered, "Where are the guards?"

Hannon rubbed his chin in thought. "Wrong hour for shifts to be changing," he muttered and shrugged. "Still, it is to our advantage. Come on."

The captain slipped out of the kitchen and walked cautiously towards the end of the hall. Torches had been doused, leaving much of the keep in shadows. Anwyn stayed as close as he could, minding where he planted his feet, still fretting the place was too deserted. Were it not for his promise to Larana, he would have turned back and fled. But Hannon was moving more swiftly through the maze of halls now, and Anwyn knew he had to keep up or get lost.

Twists and turns and stairs took them into one of the towers. At the top of the stairs, they reached a half-circle of an antechamber with an archway, and through that Anwyn could see a pair of corridors going off in opposite directions. Again, there were no guards, and Anwyn was hard pressed to not look over his shoulders, fearing this was a trap. *Why are there no guards?* The Highlord of Nymbaria would have had at least two at the head of the stairs and another at his door, as well as an attendant whose duty was to be ready to serve should the Highlord require anything in the night. It just didn't make sense.

Hannon stopped just under the archway, pointing to the corridor off to the left side.

"Her Ladyship's rooms should be that way," he whispered. "Third door to the right."

"You're not coming?"

"Better I stay out here and keep watch," he said. "Apart from which, stealing into her chamber is not a task for the Captain of the Watch. If you are what you say, you will be better off going alone."

Anwyn frowned. There was truth in that he could not argue with, though in his heart, he wondered if he had made a foolish promise. Suddenly, his whole plan was starting to look dangerous.

Stop it! he scolded himself.

He stepped cautiously down the length of the corridor, glancing back towards Hannon whose attention was on the stairs. The captain stepped back into the antechamber, disappearing from view. Anwyn stopped, wondering if he should go back. He listened, but no sound of a struggle came. *Perhaps he is just stepping closer to the stairs—in case someone does come up,* Anwyn thought to reassure himself. He continued onward. Reaching the third door to the right, Anwyn leaned an ear against the wood.

The sound of snoring was audible.

Taking a deep breath, Anwyn put a hand to the door. In his mind, he was going over the notes of his Sleep Song, ready to sing them should there be a servant inside, but as he pushed the open, it showed no resistance. Peering through the gap, he gave his eyes time to adjust to the shadows.

The chamber was long and narrow with the far wall following the curve of the tower. Moonlight was sifting through the pane glass windows, slashing the dark with milky-white light and dividing the chamber into shadows and brilliance. Half in its light, Anwyn saw a large bed with four posters and velvet drapes. The odor of mildew bit his nose. Even here, the damp was making itself known.

The middle of the bed jutted upward like a mountain that shuddered, rising and falling with each snore. Blessing his father for the gamekeeper's lessons at the skill of stealth, Anwyn stepped over to the side of the bed.

Lady Rena's face was bathed in darkness, but he could still make out the pudgy features now sagging into the pillows. He stepped closer to the bed, peering at her slack mouth, drool crawling out of one corner and smearing the silk pillow. Fighting the urge to grimace at the grotesque sight, he looked around for her jewelry. She was not wearing any at the moment. Still, he knelt to make certain the eye pendant was not on her person.

No sign of it. He stood upright and started peering around. There were bits and bobs of dangly earrings and bangles and rings strewn on the stand by the bed, but even as he carefully poked among them, he saw no sign of the pendant.

Where could it be?

He was about to draw back and look elsewhere, when he spied a bit of ribbon dangling from under one of the pillows and over the edge of the bed. Cautiously, he knelt and took hold of it, pulling slowly. Its length had some weight on the end, and it snagged a little, forcing him to carefully push his hand under the pillow. His probing fingers found the edge of hardness. Grasping it more firmly, he pulled it free.

The pendant with the emerald at the center of the pewter eye rewarded his gaze. *Thank the Four!* He didn't even have to use his magical song.

He took a deep breath and started to turn...

A meaty hand latched hold of his wrist before he could even pull away. Anwyn gasped, nearly losing his grasp on the pendant just as Lady Rena opened her eyes to glare at him.

"I've caught you now!" she said before she shouted, "Guards!"

FIFTEEN

Panic filled Anwyn. He jerked back, trying desperately to pull free, but the grasp on his arm was as ironclad as any seasoned archer's bow hand. Lady Rena made more than two of him in size as well, and she was just as determined not to let him go.

"Guards!" she shouted again. "Guards!"

Her hair danced around her face, adding to the maniacal expression. Anwyn jerked harder, losing his footing on the reed-strewn floor and sliding down into a sitting position. He braced his heels against the bed frame and pushed as hard as he could, and the action nearly dragged her out of the bed on top of him. So in desperation, he stopped pulling and pushed against her instead. She flailed in her off balance position, but still her grip prevailed, and he feared he would be forced to draw his small dagger and cut himself free.

But in the midst of twisting and jerking in the hopes of breaking her grasp, he realized a far less deadly weapon lay at hand.

"Let go!" he cried, and he grabbed one of the pillows on the bed and pummeled her with it.

Lady Rena shrieked. The attack, soft as it was, caught her by surprise. She let go to raise hands to defend her head from the feathery bludgeoning, and Anwyn suddenly found himself tumbling backwards, landing hard on the floor. The pendant flung past his head and landed in the reeds. He rolled over, scrambling on all fours like a beast, determined to claim the pendant and his freedom.

Just as Anwyn pounced on the pendant, Lady Rena shrieked once more. He turned in time to see her massive body airborne, flying at him. By the Four, she would crush him if she landed on him. He yelped and rolled aside just in time. She landed on the floor with a doughy flump of flesh unbound. Anwyn scrambled to his feet and charged for the door.

"Guards!" she screamed. "The thief is escaping! Stop him!"

Anwyn plunged through the opening, back into the corridor and stumbled into the far wall. He floundered for balance, managing to get his feet and legs turned in the general direction his body wanted to follow, and dashed madly towards the archway. Lords and Ladies, he certainly hoped Hannon was there to lead him out of this place.

He skidded through the opening, the pendant smacking his hand with its weight. Captain Hannon was nowhere to be seen. By the Four, where had he gotten himself to? Anwyn searched around, but there was no time to wait. He could hear footsteps on the stairs, a small army of men with halberds ascending towards the antechamber, blocking his path.

Cursing under his breath, Anwyn backed through the arch. Lady Rena's screams filled the corridor like a banshee on the rampage. He could hear her struggling to get to the door, her lungs heaving like bellows.

That was certainly not the way to freedom.

"Halt!" someone shouted.

Anwyn chose not to, turning and bolting into the right-hand corridor. Who slept here, he had no idea. The corridor mirrored the one containing Lady Rena's chambers, and Anwyn could only guess the Lord of Stonegorge probably occupied the other end.

At the far end of the corridor, Anwyn saw a narrow window. If he could get through it before they caught him...

He was mere meters away when an armored figure with a halberd stepped into his path. Anwyn slid to a stop with a shriek. The rest were coming up behind him. He would have to sing his gate song before...

The armored figure reached out and snagged his arm and flung him on around towards the window before he could even open his mouth and sing.

"Go, I'll hold them off!" a familiar voice boomed from within the armor.

Hannon? Anwyn shook his head. "You must come with me. They will kill you for helping me!"

"Go!" Hannon roared back. "I gave Olena my word I would look after you. Now go!"

He practically shoved Anwyn towards the narrow window, barely in time to turn and meet the first man in the charge of guards. There was a clatter of steel and staff. Anwyn backed away from the battle, uncertain what to do. But then the numbers began to push Hannon back towards Anwyn, and he had no choice but to clamber into the window opening and push through.

It overlooked a balcony, a mere few meters drop below. Anwyn steeled himself and jumped, landing and remembering to roll. He slammed into the outer railing, grabbing it for support and leaning over the edge.

Below in the dark, he could still hear the roar of the river and see the glitter of torches. The distance was too far to crawl or climb down. He would have to find another way.

"He's down there!" someone screamed from the opening above. Anwyn glanced up in time to see Lady Rena trying to wedge her head into the window gap. One arm was flailing and pointing at him.

They must have captured Hannon.

Anwyn looked down at the wall below where there stood a set of doors. He rushed at them, hoping they were unlocked.

No such luck. Backing away from them, he heard men shouting to cut him off before he escaped.

Like I can? he thought in desperation, looking around for another path. There was none.

He had no choice but to sing his Gate Song.

Inside, the thunder of many booted feet approached the doors.

Anwyn threw back his head. Finding the notes of his spell song, he sang them, concentrating on the common room of the Waterhouse Inn. The doors burst open just as the whorl of darkness swallowed him. He held his breath, barely hearing the startled gasps before that void enveloped him and opened again to spit him out. He landed on his feet, but the exertion was enough to tumble him to his knees as he drew a sharp breath of air.

There was a scream, Olena's voice.

Anwyn closed his eyes and bowed his head, fighting nausea.

"By the stones of this bridge, what are you?"

Anwyn looked up and discovered Olena standing over him, her face white.

"Mistress, I am sorry," Anwyn said. "I had no choice. It was a trap. Hannon tried to stop them—he forced me to leave without him. I don't know if he is alive or dead, but he fought bravely so I could escape."

Olena put a hand to her heart and shook her head. "They have him? But Lady Rena will kill him."

"I wanted to save him," Anwyn said. "Really, I would have if I had been able."

"Why could you not bring him here as you brought yourself?" she insisted.

Anwyn felt his own emotions welling. "I wanted to. But he pushed me away. He told me to flee. I would have brought him back, had I been able, I swear."

Olena turned away, agony filling her face. "I should never have allowed either of you to carry out this mad plan," she whispered.

"Did you find my eye?" Larana asked.

Anwyn looked over and saw the old mage woman desperately feeling her way through the common room. He took a deep another breath and opened his hand. The strap of the pendant had become wound tightly around his aching fist. But it was there, the pewter pendant, shining up at her like a beacon. Her fingers stretched and almost instinctually took hold of it. He quickly untwisted the strap and let go as she drew it from his hand. Closing her eyes, she pulled the strap over her head.

A calm overtook the room. Larana opened her eyes and looked at Anwyn with those unseeing silver orbs, and as he had often experienced when in Rhystar's company, her gaze seemed to sink into his soul. He could feel the magic working through the pendant; feel the power in this woman's heart and soul.

She smiled, lifting his chin, and said, "I was right. You are a handsome lad."

Anwyn closed his eyes.

Olena had seated herself at one of the tables, hand over her mouth. Anwyn drew out of Larana's grasp and slipped into the bench beside Olena.

"Please," he said. "You must believe I will do what I can to save him. When I have slept, I will have my spell again, and I will go back for him."

She managed a bitter smile from under her hand, and then she lowered it so she could clasp both of them in her hands.

"Hannon can take care of himself," she said softly. "I'm certain he will be fine. I am certain he will escape."

Her gaze shifted to Larana.

"You have what you came for," Olena said.

Larana nodded.

"Then do what you must to stop the river from tearing our homes from beneath us, and let it be done soon."

"I will," Larana said. "First I must..."

Her words were shattered as a fist thundered against the inn's main door.

"Open up!" a voice shouted, and Anwyn had no doubt that it was Gordon the Watchman who slammed a heavy truncheon against the wooden structure repeatedly.

"Lords and Ladies, how did he get down here so fast?"

"The baskets—assuming he ever left this level," Olena said.

"Open up in the name of the Lord of Stonegorge!" Gordon shouted, and now other voices could be heard in his wake. "Open up or I shall order the guards to break down this door!"

"You must hide," Olena said. She pushed Anwyn out of his seat and towards the back of the common room. "Fetch your harp and leave now."

"I can't," Anwyn said. "My spell is limited. I..."

"Then take your harp and go to the cellar, for it is the only place they will not dare look."

"But the water," Anwyn said.

"The top steps are still clear," she insisted. "Get your harp!"

Anwyn rushed back to the chamber where he had left Glynnanis.

:*It's about time you got back*, the harp snarled. :*I've had dreams of drowning!*

Anwyn resisted the urge to say he had considered it. The harp would just get annoyed. Besides, he could hear heavy weights pummeling the doors of the inn. Uncertain, he rushed back to the common room, the cerecloth sack and his satchel clutched close. Olena motioned for him to step behind the bar. There she had lifted a door in the floor, pointing into the dark.

He could see water lapping the stone stairs just a few meters down. Dark agitated water that roiled like an ocean tide and crested across the surface of stone.

:*We are not going in there, I hope!* an angry note ran inside his head.

Anwyn winced in pain. *We have no choice, it seems*, he thought.

"Go!" Olena said. "We will be fine."

She practically shoved Anwyn into the opening. He crouched, keeping just above the water as she dropped the door over him, and left him in watery darkness with the rankness of moisture and his own fear burning in his nostrils.

SIXTEEN

:A bit of light would be welcome right now, Glynnanis said.

But not safe, Anwyn thought in reply. His eyes were barely adjusting to the faintest bits of light slipping through cracks overhead and glittering on the restless water. The boards over him shuddered with the continual battering. He heard the snap of wood when the bar across the main door gave way, and the multitude of men marching was thunder on his sensitive ears. But he dared not cover them, not if he wanted to hear. The wood and water muffled much, but he could still hear what was being said.

"Where is the thief?" Gordon snarled.

News apparently travels faster than I thought it could.

"We do not harbor thieves here in the Waterhouse Inn," Olena retorted. "Try over at the other end of the Depths where you were born."

"You may not harbor thieves, madam," Gordon said, "but you clearly harbor traitors, for you are one yourself, you and that Captain."

"What do you mean?" Olena asked.

"I mean the Lady of Stonegorge was not pleased to learn her own Captain of the Watch has conspired with you and a witch man to bring about the destruction of Stonegorge. I have orders to bring all the traitors to Lady Rena to face justice. If you do not come willingly, then Captain Gordon will be dropped from the highest walls of Stonegorge."

Olena gasped and whimpered, "No!"

But then the thump of a staff crossing floor at a determined pace echoed from above.

"Justice? From that one, justice is a poison," Larana said. "Go back and tell my wayward daughter I will never want to see her again."

"Your daughter?" Gordon said with a snort. "Who is this mad woman?"

"She is a guest and you will treat her with respect," Olena said.

"If she is a guest, then she's probably a traitor as well. Where is the harper?"

"He's gone," Olena said. "He used his magic and fled like a coward when he heard you at the door. How did you get down here so swiftly, by the way?"

"I didn't. I've been here all along, waiting for word from my spy, and he tells me your little harper friend came back here."

"Little spy?" Olena's puzzlement was clear in her voice. "So that's what Linden spoke to you about? How dare you bribe one of my staff?"

"Didn't take much," Gordon said. "You lot, search the rooms, just in case she is lying. As for you ladies—you're coming with me. Take them both."

Anwyn clutched the straps of the harp sack and satchel so tight, his hands stung. *Lords and Ladies, what should I do?* Boots stamped back and forth, doors slammed. Olena's protests and Larana's angry words died in the distance.

He was seriously thinking of climbing back out and letting Gordon take him instead when the water began to churn. Anwyn froze, staring at the bubbling concoction that centered the cellar and drove bits of flotsam and jetsam flittering about. Slowly, a shape rose out of the middle of the chaos, gathering water into a female torso that he could see through.

And then she opened her eyes.

:*I think we better leave!* Glynnanis suggested.

But as Anwyn tried to push up the door, someone stepped on it from above. The weight and sudden jar slammed him down on the steps. He almost lost his grip on Glynnanis. The harp's strings jangled in protest and he grappled to keep it from tumbling into the water below.

"Hey, what was that?" someone shouted.

The creature's gaze shifted from him to the boards. The wraith elongated her shape into that of a snake.

Someone yanked the door over Anwyn up. "I found him!" they shouted.

Anwyn cringed as hands descended to snatch him out of the cellar.

But they never reached him.

The water wraith lunged like a viper, her silky wet surface barely skimming over Anwyn as she struck the guard full in the face. The man coughed and fell, but he could not escape her. She shoved her damp essence down his throat, drowning him.

Water splattered everywhere. Anwyn heard men shouting in terror as the wraith spread her damp presence into globules of water that sprang at the men. He raised his head out of the cellar in time to see them fall as she drowned them all. Then like some sea creature with tentacles, she gathered herself together, hovering in the air like a grotesque apparition. The guards who had not felt her wrath were fleeing out the door of the Waterhouse.

She then lowered herself to the floor where her liquid spread and washed back towards Anwyn and the cellar in a wave. He sprang out of the opening, scrambling to find purchase on the kegs and stores behind the bar. She flooded over the top of the bar, rushing back into the cellar.

Anwyn froze as she once more took on the female shape and rose to meet his gaze.

"Thank you," he muttered, uncertain what else to say.

"Where is Larana?" a voice gurgled.

"You speak," Anwyn said.

"This surprises you, mage?" she asked in turn. "You think me mere water?" Her eyes blinked coquettishly, and a wicked smile spread across her liquid lips.

Anwyn shook his head. "I'm sorry—I'm not really a true mage," he said. "I fear I have little knowledge of the ways of your kind. Forgive me." A lie, he knew, and he hoped she would not know the difference.

"Where is Larana?" she repeated.

"I think Gordon must have taken her to Lady Rena."

The wraith actually spat on the floor and shook her translucent head. "Speak not that name. She is called Tarena, and she is no lady."

"So I've noticed, Anwyn said.

"You must go to my mistress. She has the eye, but not my heart stone. You must set her free. You have the power."

"But I've already used my gate song," Anwyn said.

"You have other magic," the wraith said.

Anwyn sighed and nodded.

"Then save her—please?"

He nodded again. "I'll do what I can," he said.

The water wraith slowly slid back into the cellars. "I will be waiting," she said.

Only when she was out of sight did Anwyn relax.

Lords and Ladies, he thought. *What am I going to do now?*

SEVENTEEN

Anwyn did not dare take the baskets topside. More than once, he had been forced to detour from the sight of watchmen and guards. His desire to find a path was growing desperately slim. Gordon must have planted watchmen and guards nearly everywhere in the Depths.

Uncertain what to do, Anwyn crouched at one of the openings. He wished he were more familiar with the Depths.

"Sir? Are you lost?"

Anwyn nearly fell as he turned towards the voice. It was the urchin who had offered to lead him to the Waterhouse Inn the first time.

"Are you lost?" the lad repeated.

Anwyn shook his head. "Just unable to get topside," he said.

"Why would you want to go there?"

"To rescue a couple of friends," Anwyn said and sighed.

The boy cocked one eyebrow. "Mistress Olena?" he asked.

"Yes," Anwyn said.

"She's always been good to me, that one. Feeds me for nothing if I do a few chores."

"Yes, she is a good woman," Anwyn agreed, carefully eyeing the distance to one of the sets of stairs.

"I saw that brute Gordon and the guards forcing Mistress Olena and another woman into the baskets," the lad said. "Where was he taking her?"

Anwyn took a deep breath. "I fear he takes her to her doom for helping me," he said.

"That Gordon is a real rotten one," the lad said with a snarl.

"On that we agree," Anwyn said. "But from the looks of things, I am not going to be able to save her unless I can get up the stairs."

"Oh, you don't have to take those stairs," the lad said. "There's another way."

"You mean there are stairs they do not know about?" Anwyn asked.

"Oh, aye," the lad replied. "They did not fill them all in."

"That's worth a brass tupin then," Anwyn said. He dug into his scrip and pulled out a coin, and handed it to the lad. The lad's eyes grew as round as the tupin as he stare at it lying in the palm of his hand. Then quick as a wink, he stuffed it into his ragged scrip and gestured for Anwyn to follow.

They twisted and turned through paths Anwyn felt certain he had never seen even when he was wandering lost before. The cobbles were even more broken, and the walls dripped water in abundance.

At length, the lad took Anwyn into a seedy looking alley so narrow he was forced to turn sideways to get through. The end opened out under an arch built close into the cliffs. Moonlight sparkled on the water and cut a white swatch. Here there was an old door in the side of the arch, neglected over time. The boy helped Anwyn find a torch and get it lit, and then gave him directions.

"It goes all the way to the top and opens out just back of the gatehouse between the wall and the top arch," the boy said. "Be careful to look before you open the door, as sometimes the guards come back there to take a piss off the bridge for sport."

Anwyn assured the lad he would remember that, and for the extra information, he gladly paid five copper pats. The lad was nearly in tears as he clutched the coins tight and disappeared back into the maze.

"I just hope I don't have to come back this way," Anwyn muttered. "I don't think I will be able to find my way out."

He stepped through the doorway, pulling the waterlogged wood shut in his wake and raised the light over his head. Circular stairs greeted his gaze, rising in a spiral.

:*Not the most attractive way*, Glynnanis sang in his head.

Nor the widest, Anwyn realized quickly. He had to move his satchel and the harp sack behind him just to make the narrow ascent. It was long and grueling and took time, and more than once, he was forced to stop to catch his breath. And because of the way it was built, he had no idea how far he had come, for he long ago stopped counting the steps.

He passed other doors on the way, all embedded back in narrow niches. As tempting as it was to step through one, he forced himself to keep to his purpose. Besides, there were times he thought he heard voices. Some sounded angry, while others sounded cajoling.

Anwyn made up ditties to pass the time, and on occasion, Glynnanis sang in his head. The stairs continued to rise forever. At one point, he started to doubt there was an end. Maybe they just continued through the roof and on into the cliffs. It was hard to be certain.

But then, he made the final turn, his legs feeling like liquid and lead beneath him. The climb ended in a small chamber facing yet another wooden door.

He placed his torch in a sconce and leaned against the wall near it, and slid down to sit. *Lords and Ladies, I shall never recover.* His lungs ached and his legs were sore. How could he possibly rescue anyone in this state?

And as he sat there, he closed his eyes. And much to his chagrin, he fell asleep, dreaming of water and stone, and of the sheen of power coating everything around him. When he opened his eyes again, he saw his torch had gone out and another source of light filtered through the tiny gaps in the wooden door.

Daylight.

By the Four, he had slept too long!

He scrambled to his feet remembering the warning the lad had given him. Pressing an ear to the door, he heard nothing. He carefully pushed it open.

Somewhere in the distance over the roar of the river he heard voices. A herald? No, it was a woman, her voice full of anger, who boomed out over the crash of water and the murmur of a crowd.

Anwyn pulled his hood over his head and pushing the cover over Glynnanis, he stepped carefully out of hiding.

He recognized the area on which he stood; he was close to the gate he had left Stonegorge by. He stood on the side across from the garrison, the side where the baskets rose and fell, the side where he had escaped the palace last night.

A crowd was gathered in the open area of the bridge, and all eyes were looking upward as he worked his way into their midst. The bright coats of the watchmen of Stonegorge were everywhere, and he did his best to avoid them. Garrison guards were there as well, but it seemed to Anwyn that palace guards were holding them back.

"...We are not fools here," the woman roared. "It is clear to His Lordship and Myself who is responsible for the ill times that have befallen us. These traitors have conspired against us, and they have brought witch folk among us to destroy our beautiful bridge."

Anwyn reached an angle that allowed him a better view and froze. The woman who spoke was standing on a balcony above their head. Lady Rena had garbed herself in all her finery, and she was making sure everyone could see her by standing on a platform that lifted her above the railing.

From the edge of her platform extended four stout wide planks of wood and on three of those stood three all too familiar blindfolded. Olena and Larana stood on the outer planks, while Hannon occupied one of the inner planks.

"Liar!" one of the garrison guards shouted, and Anwyn recognized him as Sergeant Throm. "Captain Hannon has never been a traitor!"

"Silence!" Lady Rena shouted. "Your Captain may yet earn his reprieve if the real leader of this rank of traitors will but reveal himself. Otherwise, the captain will join the fate of the witch woman and the other traitor."

"Don't listen to her!" Hannon suddenly barked. "She lies!"

"Silence traitor! We know you are under the spell of the one who came here to destroy us all"

:*I think she means you*, Glynnanis said.

As if I needed to be told that, Anwyn thought in dismay. *But I didn't come here to destroy anyone!*

One of the watchmen passed him by mere inches. Anwyn managed not to flinch at the sight of the man who raked a glance about as though searching.

They are looking for me! They must know I will come here to see if I can rescue the others.

:*Of course, they know*, Glynnanis retorted. :*And if you were a real mage like Larana, you would be able to rescue them anyway.*

That thought did not cheer Anwyn in the least. He glanced casually at other members of the crowd and was relieved to see a number of them had their hoods drawn against the cold air sweeping up from the river below. At least he did not look out of place. Still, his guise would not keep him safe for long. As it was, when Anwyn glanced back at the men of the garrison, he saw Sergeant Throm peering at him in a puzzled manner.

I need a plan, Anwyn thought and turned away from Sergeant Throm's gaze.

He peered intently at Lady Rena. A bit of green and pewter glittered around her neck. Lords and Ladies, she had Larana's eye. No wonder the old woman had not been able to cast a spell in her own defense.

Anwyn glanced towards the garrison. No one was on duty there.

All the men were in the crowd, protesting the punishment of their captain.

The route to the kitchen was there...

Anwyn backed away and started towards the garrison, keeping his movements steady. He did not want to draw attention to himself.

He needed to get into the palace, and get to that window below the planks. So he moved along, eventually reaching the edge of the crowd. One quick look back and he slipped out of their numbers and into the great archway. At the far side was the entrance to the garrison.

There was no one about. Anwyn hurried across to the door on the far side and quickly made his way to Captain Hannon's chambers. To his relief, the door was not locked. He pushed it open and stepped inside, crossing the chamber to the place where Hannon had opened the secret passage to the kitchen in the palace above.

"Which stone," he muttered. His hands pressed one after another in vain. "It has to be one of these. It has to!"

:*Anwyn, have care!*

Anwyn shook his head. "It has to be one of these!" he muttered.

"One what?" a voice snarled.

Anwyn froze as a length of steel touched his throat. He shifted his eyes up its silvery length at the face of the young guardsman, Sergeant Throm.

EIGHTEEN

"What in the name of the Depths are you doing here?" Sergeant Throm demanded. "Answer me quick before I slit your throat myself!"

Anwyn took a deep breath and swallowed, staring at the blade wavering before his eyes. "I came to rescue them," he said.

"What?"

The sword withdrew a few inches so he could relax—a little.

"I came to rescue Captain Hannon and Larana and Olena," Anwyn said.

"Really?" Sergeant Throm said. "And why should I believe you?"

"Because Lady Rena is the real problem here," Anwyn said. "She bleeds the coffers dry and forces all of you to fill her wishes. She wants the Depths flooded, and she is the one who set the Water Lady down there to kill people in the hopes of driving them all out of the Depths.

Sergeant Throm lowered his sword and stepped back. "Why would she want the Depths empty?" he asked.

"Look, it would take too long to explain everything," Anwyn said. "Larana is actually Lady Rena's mother. The Water Lady is a water wraith. Lady Rena ran away from home because she was never as good at magic as her mother, and she came here to make her fortune, but she is greedy and is doing so at the expense of all of Stonegorge. Captain Hannon was helping me restore Larana's pendant, which Lady Rena stole. Larana needs that pendant to find the heart stone and stop the Water Lady from killing those who dwell in the Depths. Now I must get into the palace and see if I can stop Lady Rena before she kills them."

Sergeant Throm took a deep breath. "I was born in the Depths, and orphaned there when the rivers rose one year and swamped the nets and stole my father and mother and brother away," he said. "Captain Hannon caught me trying to pilfer his scrip. He could have tossed me to the watchmen, but instead, he brought me here and trained me, and has been like a father to me. I will not see him harmed. But I swore an oath to the Lord of Stonegorge, to protect it from traitors and those who would destroy it. How can I disobey that oath?"

:*Ask him if he swore that oath to the Lady as well*, Glynnanis said.

"Did you swear to Lady Rena as well?" Anwyn asked.

Sergeant Throm furrowed his brows. "Well, no. Not as I recall."

"Then you would not be breaking your oath to Lord Maladar of Stonegorge if you helped me rescue Hannon and Olena and Larana from Lady Rena," Anwyn said carefully. "Would you?"

He held his breath in anticipation of the answer. Sergeant Throm looked aside, a youth looking uncertain and angry. He sheathed his sword and shook his head.

"No, you are absolutely right," he said. "What can I do to help?"

"Well, first I must find the stone that opens this passage into the palace," Anwyn said, putting his attention back on the wall.

"It's this one," Sergeant Throm said. He stepped over to one side and pressed a place in the wall. The section slid open.

"Thank you," Anwyn said and started to step through.

Sergeant Throm was suddenly on Anwyn's heels, following him into the stairwell with a lantern.

"I'm coming with you," Throm said. "You have the look of a man who could use a good sword at his back."

:And he has the look of a man who has just the right sword for you, eh? Glynnanis teased in Anwyn's head.

Anwyn felt his cheeks warm. "Yes, it would be good to have someone to help me," he said. *Especially since I cannot always rely on a certain saucy harp! I'll get you for this later, Glynnanis.* The temptation to wring Glynnanis' neck was only quelled by the knowledge it was probably impossible to strangle wood.

:You wish, the harp said.

"Are you all right?" Throm suddenly asked.

"I'm fine," Anwyn replied, grateful for the shadows to hide his face. "Have you used this passage before?"

Throm hesitated. "Well, yes, though neither I nor any other guardsman of the garrison is supposed to know about it."

Anwyn nodded. He started to climb the long rise of stairs, hoping his legs would not give out considering how far he had climbed the night before. Throm stayed just far enough back to keep from setting Anwyn's cloak and hair on fire, so the shadows were leaping ahead of Anwyn when he reached the top of the stairs. Cautiously, he leaned against the wall.

The kitchen was a hive of activity now. Voices could be heard. "She'll want her supper as soon as the traitors fall," someone said.

Good, they haven't been pushed off yet, Anwyn thought.

He glanced at Sergeant Throm who mouthed, 'Leave this to me.'

Throm pushed the stone that opened the wall. It slid inward as before, revealing the fireplace hearth and the kitchen. Everything was a bustle. So at first, no one seemed to notice Throm as he stepped. Anwyn came close behind, drawing his hood to shade his silver eyes, and keeping his cloak bundled around him to disguise his Thuathyn clothes.

The vast expanse of a head cook was the first to turn. "Hoi, what are you doing here?"

"Just enjoying the smell," Throm said. "Is that pork?"

The cook furrowed two great fuzzy brows into one. "What's that hiding behind you? Some doxy?"

"My sweetheart is not a doxy," Throm said, and he pulled an arm around Anwyn's shoulders, drawing him close. "Now if you'll excuse us, we're going to miss the execution of those nasty traitors."

The cook merely frowned and motioned for them to go on. Anwyn felt his face warm again. *Lords and Ladies, was I just mistaken for a lass?*

:*I suspect it wouldn't be the first time,* Glynnanis teased. Anwyn bit his tongue rather than tell the harp to sod off. Still, Glynnanis chuckled inside his head, and Anwyn's face continued to burn.

Throm kept a firm arm around Anwyn until they were well out of the kitchen. Only then did the young sergeant whisper, "Sorry, but it was too good of a distraction."

Anwyn merely nodded. "Which way to the window under the balcony?" he asked, hoping his color would stop being so crimson.

"This way, I think," Throm said.

He took the lead. Anwyn followed. They wound their way through the nearly deserted halls. Nearly all the household, save the cooks, were out watching the 'traitors' being humiliated.

In no time, they found the windows Anwyn sought. He had seen them when he was being led into the audience hall, and when he and Hannon were dancing about the dark seeking Lady Rena's chambers. Now they rose before him, shadowed by the balcony above and the extension of wood where four wide planks extended far beyond the lip of stone.

"Now what?" Throm asked.

Now what, indeed, Anwyn thought. He still didn't have a serious plan. But with handsome young Throm standing there looking serious, Anwyn knew he had to think of something.

If he could think at all.

:*Well, it would seem to me the best thing would be to sing one of your songs,* Glynnanis suggested. :*Water, perhaps.*

Water? Anwyn frowned and glanced down towards the rage of the river so far below. Can I call water from so far?

"Well?" Throm said. "Whatever you are going to do, we'd best make haste before the patrols change."

Anwyn nodded. "Can you go up and be ready to snatch the others off the planks?" he asked.

"What are you going to do?"

Anwyn took a deep breath. "I am going to sing to the water," he said.

"And what good will that do?" Throm asked testily as Anwyn opened the window and leaned out to look at the dizzying distance.

"Just be ready to grab them," he said.

Throm nodded and slipped away.

Anwyn stared at the distance. So far. Could he call water so far?

Only one way to find out.

He waited just long enough for Throm to get into position at the door above, then taking a deep breath, and concentrating on the moisture, Anwyn opened his mouth and began to sing.

NINETEEN

As the Song of Water rushed from Anwyn's lips, the world around him trembled. There was so much water in the air, the stones of the keep and the bridge, that his summoning caused everything to shake and weep moisture.

Outside, he heard screams of fright and shouts of terror filling the air. He tried to ignore the sounds, concentrating on the water below, willing it to rise.

And rise it did, rushing upward like a geyser. The sound was like thunder, battering his ears and assailing his body, but still he sang. Water squelched beneath his feet, and started rushing down the walls. Lords and Ladies, was the whole keep composed of moisture.

The shaking grew hard enough to make it difficult for Anwyn to stand, so he grabbed the sill of the window and continued to sing. The water was almost up to the level of the top of the bridge now. He could hear panic in the cries of the men and women who had come to watch the execution, aware they fled and surged away from the balconies and lips and streets in fear the water was about to wash over the top of the bridge.

Somewhere over it all, he heard Lady Rena screaming in rage. "Find the witch man!" she said. "Find the harper!"

Feet thundered above him. Anwyn glanced up in time to see the boards bending and flexing. By the Four, where was Throm? Had he failed to reach them in time?

The water was almost even with his eyes when he heard Glynnanis shout, :*Have care!* and felt pain. Something slammed hard into his knees, knocking him down and breaking his song apart. He struggled to keep from falling backwards and crushing his harp. Glynnanis sang hearty protests of outrage as hands seized Anwyn and dragged him back from the window, yanking him around.

She stood there, glowering, her clothes dripping with moisture, her eyes full of the fire of hatred and rage.

"Throw him out the window. Now!" Lady Rena screamed.

"No!" Anwyn cried.

They did not bother to deprive him of his satchel or the harp sack. They merely dragged him back to the window. He kicked and struggled in vain, knowing full well he would never have the strength to stop them. Wordlessly, they lifted him like a sack of grain held at four corners and pitched him through the window.

He knew first the sensation of falling, of leaving his stomach behind. A scream of terror broke from his throat as he plummeted past the various levels of the bridge. The sight was little more than a blur of motion, shapes moving into masses of color.

:*Sing, damn you!* Glynnanis' voice broke through his panic like stone through glass. :Sing before it is too late!

"Sing what?" he shouted, his throat raw with pain, fear clawing at every inch of his being.

:*Air! Wind! Something to give you wings!* the harp replied.

Wind!

Anwyn closed his eyes, letting go of his fear, dragging the Song of Wind from his mind and pushing the notes over his vocal chords.

A powerful gust of air suddenly caught him, and like a leaf, he was pushed upward. As he felt himself rising, he opened his eyes and concentrated on the boards that jutted from the balcony on the keep. His body continued to rise, and he shifted around, attempting to get himself into a position that felt more comfortable. His wind bore him upward, and he once more heard screams, and someone shouting, "He can fly!"

Anwyn ignored them, directing his wind so he reached the boards just as Throm was untying Captain Hannon's bonds. Larana and Olena were rubbing their wrists. At the sight of Anwyn flying onto the balcony, Olena gasped. The others turned and stared at him as he landed near them.

"You *are* a witch man!" Throm said.

The crowd below was yammering so loud, it almost covered the sound of the falls. People were pointing and making noises of wonder.

Someone banged against the doors. Throm had taken the precaution of running a stout polearm through the handles, but now Anwyn could see the faces of guards, and among them, Lady Rena screaming in rage.

"I don't care! Break them down! Just get me that harper. Now!"

"What now?" Hannon said. "There's no way down."

"There is a way down," Larana said. "Take me to the edge."

Anwyn took her by the hand. The others looked startled as he walked her out to the vast open space.

She whispered and put her hands together, and Anwyn felt the magic grow like moisture in the air. He looked down and saw the water was rushing up towards them at an alarming rate.

Glass crashed. Thom turned and brandished his sword. The guards had managed to get one of the thick panes out and were trying to work out another so they could loosen his bar.

The water suddenly rose over their heads. The crowds panicked and ran away from the edge as a face appeared, the torso of a woman made entirely of water.

"Help us," Larana said.

The water wraith held out her hands. "Come," she said, her voice like the roar of the falls.

Larana stepped forward, tugging Anwyn.

:*No wait, she's made of water, I'll warp!* Glynnanis sang frantically.

But the hand Anwyn stepped onto felt as solid as stone. He turned back to the others and shouted, "Come on! It's all right!"

The other pane of glass broke. Olena looked at Hannon then ran towards the edge of the planks. He could do nothing more than follow her. Throm hesitated, but as he saw the others mounting the water wraith's outstretched hands, he realized it was folly to stay behind and face the hordes alone. So he followed, leaping into the water wraith's grasp just as she began to descend.

Anwyn felt his stomach shrieking in protest. The water wraith took them down so swiftly, he wondered if she were planning to drop them all in the river. But just when it looked like they would land in the raging force, she slowed her descent and stopped at the lowest level of the bridge. Men and women on the stone wharf scattered and fled. Anwyn held Larana's hand and helped her onto the lip of stone. Hannon and Olena and Thom stepped off just behind them.

The water wraith shrank down, disappearing into the river just as Larana shouted, "Thank you, Rilla."

"By the Four, that was quite a rush," Throm said, staring at the river in awe.

"Of course, now we are truly trapped, you realize," Hannon said bitterly, glancing upward. "We will have to find a place to hide because you know they will be dropping down here to pay us a visit and arrest us all for treason."

"Oh, Hannon, be quiet," Olena said. She turned to Anwyn and Larana and asked, "Now what must we do?"

"We have to find the heart stone," Larana said. "I still do not have my eye, but Anwyn here can see it for me. Once I have that and Rilla is no longer bound to the river beneath the bridge, I can defeat my daughter even without my sight. Will you be my eyes, Anwyn, you and your magic harp?"

Anwyn whispered a faint, "Yes."

He hoped she was right.

TWENTY

"It has to be somewhere around the lower levels," Larana said as Anwyn guided her along the narrow passages of the Depths. "Rilla would not stay so close to this area were it not."

"Then why can't *she* find it?" Hannon asked as he followed them.

"My guess is Tarena buried it someplace the water wraith could not go."

"Seems to me, if you are able to control this water woman as you did up there, you would be able to just take her away with you so she leaves us in peace."

"Oh, that it were so simple," Larana said. "I can ask favors of Rilla because I never treated her like a slave, but I cannot command her to go with me. Like all wraiths, she will not wander far from where her heart stone is hidden, just as much to protect it as to possess it."

"Makes no sense whatsoever," Hannon said in a surly manner. "All this magic stuff makes no sense.

Anwyn tried not to frown at Hannon's rudeness. Besides, he was having a hard time imagining there was some place the water wraith could not go in this damp. *Water is her element*, Anwyn thought. And if there was one thing he was certain of, water was everywhere.

"And just where would that be?" Hannon asked. He had left Olena in Throm's care back at the inn when she refused to leave. :*It is my home*, she had insisted, and while Anwyn admired her tenacity, he had a feeling Hannon was feeling just a bit put out by it. But they needed someone familiar enough with the Depths to guide them. *And someone good with a sword in case they find us...*

"Water cannot enter fire," Anwyn said. "As a rule, you hide a heart stone inside something that is the opposite of the wraith's nature."

:*Ah, so you have been listening to Rhystar*, Glynnanis teased.

Anwyn shook his head and refused to answer.

"Not always just the opposite," Larana supplied, "though opposites are the strongest. Water cannot enter glass, for instance, so a good thick glass ball would contain the heart stone and keep Rilla from it."

"She would just pick up the glass, wouldn't she?" Hannon asked.

"If it were loose and easy to find," Larana said. "The glass might also be in a place of fire, and that would prevent her from sensing it at all."

"No glass down here, except for the old windows on some of the outer buildings," Hannon said dully. "And certainly no fire would burn hot enough to keep that water woman from drowning it."

"Exactly," Larana said. "But Rilla has stayed down around the very foundations of this bridge. So it must be somewhere in the Depths. We just have to keep looking. Anwyn, have you seen anything unusual? Sensed anything magical?"

"Sorry," Anwyn said. He had tried to look into shadows and windows, but he saw no hint of the magic that was holding the wraith prisoner. "It must be buried very deep..."

He paused...

"What?" Larana asked, stopping in her tracks to whip around towards him.

Anwyn glanced at Hannon.

"She buried it inside the bridge," Anwyn said.

"What?"

"Hannon, you told me Lady Rena had come down during the rebuilding of parts of the bridge and tossed a stone into the pile," Anwyn said.

"Well, yes, but..." Hannon shook his head. "It was just a small glassy stone. I remember the workers laughed about it afterwards and made fun of Lady Rena, saying anything bigger than her thumb would have been a strain, they imagined."

"Glassy? Like water?" Larana said, turning to Hannon as though she could actually see him.

"Yes..."

"Shaped like a tear?"

Hannon frowned. "Well, yes."

"Anwyn, you're right, I am certain of it. It would explain why Rilla refuses to leave—why she is trying to wash away the very foundations of the bridge. One place water cannot enter is solid stone."

"Where was this place?" Anwyn asked Hannon.

"Over near the inn," he said. "The old pillar where we ascended to the upper levels…"

"We have to go back there," Anwyn said, remembering the sensation he had felt while climbing those stairs.

Hannon frowned, but he turned on his heels. "Then we had best make haste," he said. "It's not going to take them much longer to get down here."

Anwyn nodded. He had been listening for the basket lifts when they were closer to the northern side, but so far, he had not heard them. Then again, considering what Rilla had done to rescue them, Lady Rena might have been having a difficult time convincing her soldiers to storm the depths.

They reached the pillars where the stone was different. There was magic here that faintly sang to Anwyn, the thrum of a low string plucked on a harp. He put a hand to the surface.

"It must be here," he said, and he reached over to guide Larana to the place. The moment her hands touched the pillar, she gasped with delight.

"Yes, it is here," she said. "We must remove these outer stones and..."

"Remove those stones and you'll likely collapse the walls," Hannon argued. "Those stones are holding up the braces that keep the stones above our heads intact."

"But they must be removed if I am to reclaim the heart stone," Larana said.

"Can't you just magic it out?"

"Mortals! You understand nothing of magic..."

How deep is it, Glynnanis? Anwyn thought.

:*No more than the length of your arm*, Glynnanis replied. :*When she threw the heart stone in, there was already a lot of stone in place.*

Is there some way to reach it with magic?

Anwyn saw Larana looking dubiously in his direction.

"If you were to change the stone to something softer," she said.

Anwyn frowned. He had already used his Song of Water and his Song of Air. So what could he use to change the stone? Lightning would shatter it. And bring down the whole bridge.

:*You could try the Song of Easing a Heart*, Glynnanis suggested. :*Or perhaps your Song of Feast.*

"Don't be ridiculous, Glynnanis, that song is for..."

:*For calling a feast to me.* Anwyn stared at the wall. The Song of Feast was a song of summoning. It summoned food, but the food had to come from a source. In the past, he had used it to sing food from Rhystar's stores.

:*Who is to say you cannot sing the stone out of the wall if you concentrate on the heart stone itself*, Glynnanis said.

Anwyn took a deep breath and closed his eyes. He concentrated on the bit of water magic he could feel buried in the wall. Humming the notes of his Song of Feast, he held forth his hand.

He heard Larana gasp in surprise, and Hannon curse like an old sailor. Anwyn ignored them both, letting the song flow from his lips, reaching for the heart stone with his mind.

And suddenly it came to him, weighty in his hand, a stone like a tear-shaped glob of glass, heavy as water in a bottle...

"I did it!" he cried and turned just as Glynnanis rang with a sharp note of warning.

There was a cudgel coming straight at Anwyn's head, and behind it he could see the blazing rage in Gordon's eyes.

TWENTY-ONE

Instincts are honed by practice. Anwyn had learned most of his in the hunting forests under his father's guardianship. As a lad, Anwyn had narrowly escaped a limb when it broke free in a high wind and lashed across at him like a backhand blow. Something had moved him then to duck under the flying chunk of wood. Now as he saw the cudgel, that same instinct came into play. He dropped low as the cudgel flashed through the air where his head had been and hit the stone of the pillar. Bits of it were shattered under the heavy metal head.

Scrambling for safety, Anwyn heard Gordon roar. Anwyn barely had time to look back at Hannon and Larana who were now in the hands of other watchmen. Gordon shouted and rushed at Anwyn like an enraged bull, rearing back for another blow. Anwyn managed to dodge again, thankful that his smaller size made him more agile than the hulking watchman. As it was, Gordon's strength was working against him, and he bounced off the wall of the narrow passage and nearly fell into the men rushing forward to assist him.

Anwyn took advantage of their jam of bodies to sprint for the nearest opening.

By the Four, he had known they would come, but he had hoped they would be delayed. Now he could hear Hannon arguing with the watchmen, trying his best to create a diversion or a delay. In either case, Anwyn knew he could not wait. So he ran, hurling himself through the twisting paths of the Depths, praying that he did not turn down one of the dead ends.

"Stop him!" Gordon shouted. "He's got the stone!"

:*Oh, wonderful, now they'll all want one*, Glynnanis sang.

Anwyn cursed as he charged out onto the northern edge of the bridge, finding himself at the platform overlooking the rush of water out of the mountains. He glanced around for the stairs, knowing full well he could not risk the basket ride. But just then, several of the guards from the palace above, with Lady Rena in the lead, came charging through the arches.

"Lords and Ladies!" Anwyn sputtered as Lady Rena fixed him with her cold stare.

"He has the stone that will kill the beast that tears down our bridge!" she cried. "Get it for me!"

At that point, Gordon and his watchmen surged out of the passageways and onto the stone docks.

"No place to run, witch man!" Gordon shouted. "Now give me the stone."

They formed a semi-circle, forcing Anwyn towards the edge. He stood, heaving from breathlessness, knowing he had no lungs left with which to sing, and no spell song that would not cause harm to these men.

:*They're going to hurt you!* Glynnanis said. :*Rhystar would wipe them all off the face of the earth and…*

I'm not Rhystar! Anwyn retorted.

"Get me that stone, Gordon!" Lady Rena said, "and I will make you the new Captain of the Guard!"

Gordon roared. He rushed forward, his cudgel of authority raised like a sword. "Give me that stone or I'll bash your head in and take it anyway."

"Then take it from her!" Anwyn retorted. He turned and flung the heart stone away from him so it arced through the air. "Rilla!" he shouted.

"No!" Gordon and Lady Rena shouted.

The heart stone glittered in the sunlight like a great diamond when the waters rose and became a woman's form. Her hand reached upward and snatched the stone from the air.

"No!" Gordon shouted and shifted his swing. Anwyn heard Glynnanis give warning and stepped aside, but the cudgel still caught him in the shoulder with bone crunching pain. His whole left arm went numb, and Anwyn staggered and screamed. He dropped to his knees, desperate to keep from crushing Glynnanis, but the pain was greater than he could bear. And Gordon was still shouting, rearing over Anwyn with a face contorted by insane fury.

"You bastard! I'll kill you for that!"

Gordon's shouts were echoed by Lady Rena's banshee scream for Anwyn's blood.

Then be quick about it, Anwyn thought, eager to escape the pain that was sending blinding flashes across his vision and making his stomach heave.

But the blow Gordon reared back to deliver never came. Water suddenly lashed up and over the edge of the stone rim and slammed into the big man. Through a haze of pain, Anwyn watched the scene unfold. Water knocked Gordon down, pouring onto him with a fury equal his own, forcing itself into his throat. His men could not do anything to save him. Indeed, they were turning on their heels and fleeing with shouts of terror.

Gordon struggled vainly against the water, but it filled him, distending him like a puffer fish, until he stopped struggling and drown.

Lady Rena was backing away. Her guards had tried to stand and protect her, but water was lashing at them, tossing them aside like small children. In desperation, Lady Rena pulled forth the eye pendant and raised it like a talisman.

"Back!" Lady Rena screamed. "Back to the river, foul fiend."

Rilla merely snarled, her face shifting from translucent beautiful to that of a monstrous fury. She threw herself at Lady Rena with a howl. The lady tried to turn and flee, but Rilla shifted to a mass of her elemental form. Water slammed into Lady Rena's back, knocking her down. Lady Rena flailed and slapped at the water that formed an orb of moisture around her. Floating in the middle, she tried to swim towards the surface in vain, but the weight of her fine clothes became saturated, dragging her to the bottom.

Anwyn wanted to shout for Rilla to release the lady, but his pain kept him from doing so. He gritted his teeth and watched as Lady Rena—once known as Tarena—opened her mouth to scream. A great gout of bubbles flooded from her throat, and then she ceased to move, floating like a leaf caught in a pool.

There was a shout that sounded vaguely like Hannon and another that sounded like Larana, but Anwyn no longer cared. He closed his eyes, pain drowning his senses so the world went away and plunged him into a damp darkness.

TWENTY-TWO

Anwyn awoke to the whisper of voices nattering nearby.

"Are you certain he will be all right?" That sounded like Olena.

"I have set the bone and called a healing spell on him," Larana said. "It is all I can do for the time."

Anwyn let his eyes flutter open. He was in a chamber that looked familiar, a room in an inn with curtained windows. Larana was seated beside the bed on which he lay. Behind her, he could see Olena with a tray.

:*He wakes*, Glynnanis sang.

"What...?" Anwyn took a deep breath. His left shoulder felt stiff as a new bow. He reached across with his other hand and touched the place where the pain had been the worse. It felt whole. "What happened?"

"More than you will know," Larana said. "Rilla saved you."

Anwyn frowned as memories flooded him. "She drowned Gordon. And your daughter."

"Yes," Larana said. "You set her free, and she could have gone away and left us to our fate."

Anwyn closed his eyes. "What will you do now?" he asked. "She has killed and..."

"I have set Rilla free. She has gone down river and taken her flood with her. Stonegorge's Depths are no longer under the threat of drowning."

"But what of the others...they know she did this. They'll harm you and Throm and Olena and..."

"I don't think so. You see, once Rilla drowned the Lady Rena, Captain Hannon supposedly killed her. I asked her to pretend to die. He cut her apart with his sword, and she did her part to fall to pieces and flow away. It was a wondrous thing to see. Those who witnessed his act of bravery were astonished he had such strength against a creature of magic and saved the city. Of course, they mourned the lady's loss, and their lord is wearing black to show his grief. And Captain Hannon had been promoted to the position of Lord's Advisor. He will begin his duties by attending the funeral of the Lady Rena and follow that by abolishing the high tariff so those who wish to cross this city under the bridge may do so once again."

Anwyn frowned, glancing at Olena. "And you?"

"I will continue to offer room and board to those who cannot afford the fancier inns above," Olena said and smiled. "Just because my husband to be is the Lord's Advisor does not mean I cannot carry on as I always have."

Anwyn smiled faintly to hear that, and Olena ducked her head.

"So, when you are feeling well enough, you can be on your way," Larana said.

"But what about you?" Anwyn asked. "Where will you go? Back to your ruins?"

"Oh, no. The Lord of Stonegorge has offered me a place here. Now that I have my sight back and my spells in order, I will be using my magic to keep Stonegorge from crumbling into the river."

Anwyn sighed. "I missed it all then," he said. "You're not angry because I gave Rilla back her heart stone, are you?"

Larana smiled and shook her head. "I had long thought I would set her free. Wraiths are so unpredictable they should not be kept in captivity. Now here, I think Olena had brought you a fine meal of broth, bread and cheese. Would you like help sitting up?"

Anwyn shook his head. Cautiously, he eased himself into a sitting position. Glynnanis was in the chair at the foot of the bed looking over the rail.

Larana placed the tray within reach and headed for the door. "I'll check in on you later," she said.

Anwyn nodded. She and Olena slipped out of the chamber and left him with his thoughts.

He tested the food and found it good, and once he had devoured all of it, he sat on the edge of the bed, looking towards the curtained window. It was open, and a breeze was fluttering the cloth.

Carefully, he pulled himself out of the bed and stepped over to the window. Pushing the drapery aside, he was greeted by the sight of the river placidly rolling down under the bridge from much farther away than he remembered before. Moonlight was casting diamonds on the water, and pearly tears of it splashed each of the shores to either side of the gorge.

"I caused it all," he muttered.

:*Not really*, a voice whispered back.

Moisture gathered before him, rising from the river below. A woman's shape, translucent in the moonlight, formed before him. He saw her smile.

:*You have my thanks, Harper Mage*, Rilla said, her voice the melodious gurgle of a brook over stones. :*I have my freedom, and I owe you my gratitude.*

The word of a wraith, Anwyn remembered Rhystar once saying, *is never to be trusted.*

Anwyn smiled.

"You owe me nothing," Anwyn said. "You saved my life, after all."

She nodded as though understanding then she fell, becoming nothing more than mist and water raining back down on the river.

He would leave tomorrow, early if he could manage it. He would sing his own Healing Song to make certain his stiff shoulder was able to work again, and then he would go.

And leave the city under the bridge behind as little more than a memory.

WolfSinger Publications
Don't Write What You Know;
Write What You Care About—
Passionately!

2009 Scheduled Releases

The City Under the Bridge – Laura J Underwood

The Hotel Galileo – Lee Moan

A Time To Volume 3 – The Best of the Lorelei Signal 2008

Arcane Whispers Volume 2 – The Best of Sorcerous Signals 2009

A Cycle of Gods – Henry Lazarus

WolfSongs Volume 2 – edited by M.H. Bonham

All About Eve – edited by Carol Hightshoe

Visit us at
www.wolfsingerpubs.com